THE NIGHTWALKER

THE NIGHTWALKER

An Eric Ward Mystery

Roy Lewis

Chivers Press   •   Thorndike Press
Bath, England   Waterville, Maine USA

This Large Print edition is published by Chivers Press, England, and by Thorndike Press, USA.

Published in 2002 in the U.K. by arrangement with Allison & Busby Limited.

Published in 2002 in the U.S. by arrangement with Allison & Busby Limited.

U.K. Hardcover   ISBN 0–7540–4923–X (Chivers Large Print)
U.K. Softcover   ISBN 0–7540–4924–8 (Camden Large Print)
U.S. Softcover   ISBN 0–7862–4254–X (Nightingale Series Edition)

The text of this Large Print edition is unabridged.
Other aspects of the book may vary from the original edition.

Set in 16 pt. New Times Roman.

Printed in Great Britain on acid-free paper.

British Library Cataloguing in Publication Data available

PROLOGUE

The early morning air was chill.

The innocuous blue van was parked at the roadside at the end of the line of decaying Victorian villas with their narrow, rankly-grassed and weed-strewn gardens. The houses were solid and gloomy, withdrawn in appearance with bay ground floor windows heavily curtained against the outside world. The area had once displayed an air of gentility, perhaps fifty or sixty years ago: that gentility had crumbled now under decay and neglect, the collapse of local industry, and the refusal of grant-aid in view of the reputation of the area for mindless violence, theft and general social abuse.

The men in the blue van sat quietly, saying nothing. One of them was smoking; since he was the most senior officer present, no objection was raised. His cigarette glowed as he inhaled: the faint light hollowed his cheeks and his eyes seemed to glitter. Detective Inspector Connelly was known to be a hard man: in his rugby playing days, not so long ago, he had tested his strength and determination against bigger men and seen them crumble. He sat quietly now, patient, drawing on his cigarette as one of the team cleared his throat, hawking aggressively.

1

A squawking noise came from the receiver in Connelly's pocket. Quickly, he recovered the mobile phone and held it close to his ear. The instructions were brief and to the point. He nodded, switched off the phone and looked around at the five men seated with him in the van. 'Back-up is in position. Newton's covering the lane behind the houses. Far end of the street is sealed. And there's no one else coming in tonight, it seems.'

There was a brief murmur, indicating disappointment and irritation. They had been waiting for almost three hours, expecting a bigger fish to enter the premises. That had been the tip-off from the informer.

'We go in now, anyway,' Connelly said quietly. His tone was low but edged with tension. He stood up, half-crouching, and peered out of the window. There was another van turning into the street. Connelly nodded. 'There's the cavalry.' At his signal, the officer at the rear of the van opened the doors, and quietly the six men stepped down, into the dark street.

The second van was purring its way quietly towards them. At the far end of the street Connelly could make out the other unit, sealing off the area. He took a deep breath, nodded and waited for a few seconds until the second van came to a halt. The men came out quickly, dark-clothed, thick-set in their body armour, armed.

'Let's do it,' Connelly said.

The gate to the small front garden had long since disappeared. Connelly led the way, then stepped to one side as the burly constable smashed down the front door. They poured into the narrow hallway, shouting: three men fanned out into the ground floor rooms, Connelly led the way to the upper floor, his feet pounding, echoing noisily on the uncarpeted stairs.

They were all yelling: the sound the result of the adrenalin and excitement rushing through their veins. Upstairs, someone else shouted, and then Connelly was standing on the landing, kicking in a bedroom door, while his team ranged through to the other rooms.

The bedroom Connelly entered was dark, heavily curtained, but there was a familiar smell in the air, and Connelly grunted with satisfaction. He heard someone swearing, a chair turned over, crashing, and the man beside him flicked on his flashlight. The beam picked up a big man, clad in sweatshirt and underpants, heavily muscled, unshaven, bleary-eyed, and swearing. The words came out in a rush of obscenity, mindless; the man's eyes were glazed with sleep, undirected as yet, but dangerous.

His intentions were clear also, from the baseball bat he held in his right hand.

The house seemed to reverberate with screams and shouts, protestations as men and

3

women were dragged from beds, swearing, pleading, and the men from the SWAT team took no chances, yelling instructions, deafening protest, manhandling people to the floor, screaming in emotions that were part excitement, part panic. They all knew what could happen: if they failed to impose terror themselves, a sudden act of bravado or stupidity could result in mayhem.

Carefully, Connelly fumbled at the wall on his left and found the light switch. He flicked it on. Suddenly, the room was bathed in a harsh, unshaded light. The man with the baseball bat raised a hand to his eyes, briefly, squinting, then lowered it. Now he held the bat in a two-handed grip.

'Now then, Danny,' Connelly said in a soothing tone. 'You don't want to do something stupid.'

'Bastard.'

The man's tone was surprisingly cool, in view of the sudden attack on the house, and the screaming and shouting that came from the other rooms.

'We got you dead to rights, old son. I can smell it in the air. Give it up: it'll only make things worse if you put up a fight. What's the point?'

'*This* is the point,' the big man sneered, gripping the club and swinging it slowly in a caricature of a sporting stance. 'You Irish bastard. Come and get your head split.'

'Now Danny, you know better than that,' Connelly suggested. 'Put that damn thing down, and let's make this a peaceable experience.' But he was smiling as he said it. He had never been a man to avoid or ignore a challenge; the street knew it, and the big man facing him knew it. Danny Blanchard had never been one to back down. But Connelly had faced a pack of rampaging forwards on the rugby field often enough and never flinched. He wasn't backing down now, either. Surprisingly light on his feet for his bulk, he charged.

The big man swung the baseball bat in a wild arc—wild, but with sufficient accuracy to catch Connelly on the upper arm. The policeman yelled in pain and muffled anger, but he was already under the swing, at close quarters and boring into the heavily muscled Blanchard the way he had bored into scrums in the old days, snarling, imposing his presence, his muscle and his will. The club flailed crazily as Connelly slammed into his opponent with his shoulder and they both went crashing across the bed into the wall beyond.

The man was big, but off balance: he was underneath Connelly and at close quarters the bat was ineffective. In a moment, as Blanchard struggled, the weapon was torn from his grasp by the officer behind Connelly, and then Connelly had his forearm thrust hard against his captive's throat. He ignored the searing

5

pain in his left shoulder as he thrust down, watching the man's eyes bulge, seeing his mouth gasp open, seeking for air. Then Connelly head-butted him, breaking Blanchard's nose with a satisfying crunch. Blood streamed from his own forehead as he raised himself up, straddling his opponent.

'Now then, who were you calling an Irish bastard?' he gritted.

He smashed his right forearm into the man's face, hearing the jaw crack. He bunched his fist into a hard, knuckled ball, and broke the nose again, so that the dark blood gushed out in a violent stream. There was a gurgling sound, but Connelly was relentless. His blood was up. Someone was dragging at his shoulder as he pounded away at Blanchard but the red mist that had descended on him drove him on. It was only when the man underneath him was limp, and two men were restraining him that Connelly was persuaded to stop.

The breath was tearing at his chest, ragged, and the blood was still raging in his head, but Connelly allowed himself to be restrained. He nodded, intimating he was under control again. The grip on him relaxed. There was an eerie silence in the house. The screaming and shouting was over, suddenly. Connelly rubbed at his arm: it wasn't broken, he knew, but it was going to give him trouble over the next week. He looked at the other two officers in the room. 'You secured all the bastards?'

6

One of them nodded. 'Seven in all. And a stack of shit. Enough to nail them for possession, and dealing as well. It was a good tip-off, sir.'

The other officer was staring at the unconscious man on the bed. He licked his lips. 'Is . . . is he going to be all right?'

Connelly grunted and smiled thinly. There was the taste of blood in his mouth. 'I know Danny of old. He knew what to expect. But he wanted to try it on. He's got a reputation to uphold. He'll need it, when he's serving time.'

'He looks pretty bad. You think we should call the ambulance?' The officer was young, inexperienced. Connelly glanced at his companion and grinned sourly. 'It was called for an hour ago.' Abruptly, he turned away. 'All right. Let's get this lot cleared out of the house. The search teams—'

'They're already busy, sir. The wagon's outside, and we're hauling them out, all seven of them, dressed or not.'

'You shouldn't treat them so roughly,' Connelly suggested ironically.

'We wouldn't want them to feel *unregarded*, sir.'

The man on the bed turned, gurgling, choking on his own blood.

'Get Blanchard down with the others,' Connelly said. Then he stood still, waiting for a few moments as the two officers lifted the injured man from the bed, and pushed him, half-supported, towards the stairway. Connelly made a brief search of the room: it was barely furnished, just the bed with its dirty sheets, and a chest of drawers. He went through them quickly. There was nothing of interest. No matter—the team had already picked up evidence of drugs.

Then Connelly waited, listening. There was something wrong. His instincts told him so. Slowly he walked out of the bedroom onto the uncarpeted landing.

He stayed at the top of the stairs. Below him the other officers tumbled their charges out to the police van. A siren started up as the ambulance arrived. The noise in the street grew, a cacophony of shouts, protests, instructions, mingled with roaring car engines. The street out there would be watching from behind their dark windows, but they wouldn't get involved. This was a drugs bust. Nothing unusual in this part of Tyneside: a bit of theatre for an hour or so, and then everything back to normal—deals, plans, night pleasures.

Connelly waited. He could not have said why he waited: there had been nothing he could have put his finger on. But he was an experienced copper, and if his gut, his instinct told him there was more to come, he was prepared to go along with it.

And in a little while, he was rewarded.

It was only a light thud, a soft footfall, barely audible. But it was enough. Connelly let out a sigh of satisfaction and shrank back into the shadows. He always enjoyed being right.

The noise had come from the back bedroom, overlooking the yard. Everything was silent again now, but Connelly knew what he had heard. He remained still, waiting, half shadowed at the top of the stairs. Several minutes passed by, but at last he thought he detected a slight movement in the half-open door to the bedroom at the far end of the corridor. The woodwork creaked slightly, the door moved again, the gap widening and as Connelly stood there he saw in the light of the naked bulb in the corridor the reddish, tousled hair of the boy peering around the door.

It was a face he knew: pale-skinned, freckled, the nose bluntly upturned. There was an arrogance about the hard blue eyes that was only slightly shaded now with caution. The boy was crouched, seeming even shorter than the five feet he aspired to and he was poised, ready to fly at any moment.

Connelly smiled in satisfaction. 'Hello, Tinker,' he said, almost amiably.

The boy started. There was a short silence. The youngster was fifteen feet away and alert, but in no way alarmed. His blue eyes gleamed as he stared at Connelly, their arrogance challenging him. His lips writhed in a grimace, a gaptoothed smile of contempt and then as Connelly moved towards him, he vanished.

The door slammed behind him and

Connelly lunged into a run. He slammed his shoulder into the door and bit back a cry of agony as the sharp pain lanced through his damaged shoulder. The door gave way, and he burst into the room. He looked around and saw the trapdoor in the ceiling, through which the boy had dropped. He would have hidden up there immediately he had heard the front door smashed in by the SWAT team. He had always been a swift, smart bastard. Connelly turned, and caught a brief glimpse of movement at the window.

He rushed forward, but he was too late. He thrust his head out of the open window. The night had been dark and cool but now a crescent moon was emerging from behind silvered clouds. In the faint light Connelly caught the movement to his left. The small, lithe figure of the boy was on the sloping roof of the house next door: unbelievably, in a matter of seconds he had crawled along the ledge outside the window, crossed to the next house and was now poised, crouching on the tiles, staring back at Connelly.

'You'll break your bloody neck!' Connelly snarled, knowing otherwise.

The boy stared at him contemptuously, then slowly raised his arm extending two fingers of his left hand in a confident, jeering, authority-despising gesture. Connelly looked around angrily, down to the back yard below and the narrow lane at the back. There was a car still at the end of the lane, but the officers there were unaware of what was happening above their heads. Connelly swore. He looked back again to the sloping roof. The boy was gone.

'Little bugger,' Connelly swore, rubbing at his injured arm.

There was no point in pursuit. The boy would be long gone by the time they started a hunt for him. As he made his way down the stairs to rejoin the team, Connelly wondered whether he should even report the sighting. It wasn't the first time the boy had escaped from police custody, or in this case, near-custody. And even when they'd had him in court, the magistrates had done sod all except reprimand him.

'Find anything else, sir?' the driver asked as Connelly got into the van. Connelly hesitated, uncertain still whether to report what had happened. He shrugged wearily. 'Nothing important,' he replied. 'Let's get on back to the nick. We got a long night ahead of us with this lot.'

Little bugger, he thought to himself.

CHAPTER ONE

1

Eric Ward stood at the window of the drawing room in Sedleigh Hall. The view was one he had always appreciated. The wide terrace and the steps leading down to the lawn opened to a vista across the meadows below; the stream that ran there held trout and attracted heron, wild deer occasionally crossed at the narrow bridge in the early morning mist, in spring the curlews sent their plaintive calls echoing to the woods, and at mating time hares danced their intricate rituals, boxing and sparring and racing each other through the short-grazed grass of the meadow. And always, in the distance, there was the slow rise of the hills up to the blue-hazed Cheviots.

He recalled how the grouse used to whirr out of the heather when he and Anne had ridden up there, their mounts pacing across the sloping fell, crossing brownflecked beck water and ridges of ancient rock; they had startled owl among the trees, heavy-flighted under the morning sun, and they had breathed air that came with the sea-tang from the distant coastline, salty in the crisp cold winter mornings when the snow came, deep, undisturbed, blanketing everything with silence.

Sedleigh Hall held many memories for him—all of them pleasurable, until recently. But a few months ago there had been a gunshot here, the web of deceit he had developed about him had begun to unravel, and his world had started to crumble about him.

He heard Anne enter the room behind him. He half turned his head, to acknowledge her presence, but he said nothing. She moved around behind him, uncertainly. After a moment she said 'What time are you leaving?'

'Shortly.'

'Are you staying overnight?'

He nodded. 'I'll be at the flat.' He hesitated. 'I've got a number of appointments this week. I'll stay on there for a while.' Lamely, he added, 'There suddenly seems to be a rush of clients.'

'That'll take your mind off things,' Anne said in a cool, constrained tone.

He turned, looked at her. He had a sudden memory of the first time he had seen her. She had been coming down the hill, through the trees above Dent's farm. The horse she rode had been a magnificent animal, sheer black, muscles rippling under its glossy coat. Anne had been wearing a riding habit; the light had cast a russet glow on her hair and he had felt immediately attracted. She was not a conventional beauty, but there was a warmth in her smile . . . it all seemed so long ago.

14

It *was* long ago, and things had changed.

She had matured, and was even more attractive now, more confident, less reliant upon his judgement. The estates her father had left her, and the business interests she had developed, they had all played their part. But she had never really understood—appreciated that he needed to live his own life, was unable to play the role she wanted for him, married to a wealthy woman. His practice on the Quayside in Newcastle had always been a bone of contention—and he had to admit that most of her circle seemed to feel the same way, unable to understand why he should want to struggle along with a criminal practice when he could be living a grander professional life, through her contacts and her business interests. But he had tried that, and it didn't work.

And now it seemed his marriage wasn't working, either.

'Will you be coming back, Eric?' she asked suddenly.

His eyes held hers. His mouth was suddenly dry and there were no words available to him.

'Because we are not . . . it just.' Her glance slipped past him, to the windows. 'I thought we had reached an agreement. I thought we both felt the past, the recent past months, were best buried. But somehow . . .'

He knew he would regret the words even as he spoke them. 'It's not only the past, Anne.

15

It's the present as well. Sullivan is still . . .
always around.'

Her lips tightened, and there was a certain
sullenness around her mouth. She made an
irritated, dismissive gesture with her left hand.
'I don't know what's got into you, Eric. Of
course, Jason Sullivan is still *around*, as you
put it. But what on earth do you expect? He
was instrumental in setting up the Singapore
business arrangements in the first instance,
and after we decided to pull out—and that was
your advice, by the way—it only made sense to
use Jason to wind everything up. After all, he
knew more about it than anyone else. And
apart from that, you *chose* to resign from
Martin and Channing, I have to have a lawyer
representing our interests on the board, Jason
is well regarded in the City and is prepared to
take it on . . . of *course* he's still around.'

He knew she was right; he knew she had
logic on her side. It had been his own choice to
resign from the board of the merchant bankers
in which she held a considerable financial
interest—because he wanted to be his own
man, run his own professional life. But the fact
she had turned to Jason Sullivan QC still
rankled. Not least because there was also the
matter of his own guilt. Marital infidelity left
emotional scars: she had not wanted the
details of his fall from grace, though she
suspected the truth. And he had agreed not to
question her about the nature of her

16

relationship with Jason Sullivan.

But it wasn't working. Slowly, insidiously, worms of doubt were gnawing at him, and they brought back the tensions that caused the cat claws to scratch again at the back of his eyes, so his nerve ends screamed and the old, shuddering pains returned in the darkness.

'I just don't see why . . .' His words trailed off lamely. They could quarrel over this, but the last thing he wanted was a quarrel. It would take them nowhere. He needed to get away from Sedleigh Hall for a few days, bury himself in work, give himself time to think things through.

'I have to go,' he said.

She made no reply.

*   *   *

He took the Celica. Normally, he enjoyed the drive from Sedleigh Hall back to Newcastle, since it crossed the fells, offering distant views of the sea at Amble, occasional pele towers, against the magnificent backdrop of the Northumbrian hills. But even though it was a fine morning, blue sky scudded with racing white clouds, he was unable to appreciate the scenery. His mind was still churning over the last few months, his stupidity at getting involved in the death of a call girl, and the violence and anxieties that had arisen out of it all.

17

Some ten miles north of Newcastle he saw the sign to Ewart Village and turned into the narrow side road. He drove past wide fields separated by earthen banks that had been planted a hundred years earlier with quickset hedges of hawthorn; the road dropped down towards the coast past woods and shelter-belts where the field boundaries were suddenly stone walls and dykes, and then the view opened out ahead of him and he could see the small village of Ewart, and some two miles beyond the scattering of buildings that was Stagshaw waste transfer station. At the top of the hill he slowed, and stopped, pulling in at a narrow layby. He got out of the car, walked over to a farm gate and leaned on it, staring down towards Stagshaw.

His files had told him that the cluster of buildings—a rundown site consisting of sheds and concrete-lined pits—had begun life a hundred and fifty years ago as a tanning factory. It had caused enough problems then, with the odours from the tanning process bringing complaints from the adjoining villages. But those days had long gone. The site had been given a new lease of life some ten years ago when the owners had sought, and been granted, licences for the storage at Stagshaw of toxic substances. Apparently, the substances included industrial solvents such as xylene and toluene, methylene chloride and trichlorethylene, and cyanide.

Just about everything, it seemed, other than nuclear waste.

Eric stood there for a while, musing, watching the slow faint drift of white smoke from the waste site, barely moving in the light breeze, drifting eastwards, towards the coast. He sighed, then got back into the car. He had an appointment with Eddie Ridout. He could see the farmland below him: the farm lay just three miles from the waste site

The farmhouse was eighteenth century in structure, nestled into the slope of a hill, protected from the north winds by a bank of trees, the end gable boasting long mullioned windows, the main section of the house fronted by a Georgian pediment, the whole structure presenting a solid, confident, yeoman face to the world. It had been in the hands of the Ridouts for five generations, Eric understood. He drove into the main yard in front of the house, and parked under a towering sycamore tree. When he got out of the car, Eddie Ridout was standing at the front door, waiting.

He shook hands gruffly, and then led Eric into the vast kitchen with its wood-burning stove, a rack of drying clothes suspended above, a pile of dirty dishes in the sink under the window. A man living alone. He gestured Eric to a seat at the long wooden table. 'Coffee?' he asked bluntly.

'Please.'

Eric watched the man as he made two mugs of coffee. Eddie Ridout was a widower, perhaps fifty years of age, solid of body, stocky in build, his head bald apart from two strips of greying reddish hair above his ears. He had the skin and wrinkled eyes of a man who had spent his life out of doors; his shoulders were broad and muscular, his hands were hard-knuckled, his fingers gnarled. He gave the impression of reined power, but it was rumoured he had an explosive temper, and had no truck with fools or weaklings. It was Eddie Ridout who was leading the protests against the waste site—and with good cause, Eric knew.

'I'm glad you could find time to come out to see me,' Ridout said in a gruff, slightly embarrassed tone, as he handed Eric his mug of coffee. 'I'd have been okay to come into Newcastle, you know.'

'I've been up at my home,' Eric explained. Somehow, the word *home* suddenly held an odd ring for him. 'It's on my way to Newcastle, coming here.'

'Aye, well . . . It's Sedleigh Hall you live isn't it? The Morcomb estates.'

'That's right.'

'I used to go shooting up there when I was a bairn. I met Lord Morcomb a few times. Sam was up there a few times, when he was younger. But he lost interest in crow-shooting. Lost interest in most things, now,' he added grimly.

Eric nodded. He had read the details on the file. Sam Ridout was in hospital. The prognosis was not good. 'I just thought it would be a good idea to talk a bit, before we get to the hearing with the other side. I've arranged for Dr Armstrong to be present: he'll give us information about the side effects of the toxic waste. But it would be useful if you and I run over now what you need to bring out in the discussions.'

'Will Lon Stanley be there?' Eddie Ridout asked, raising his mug to his lips.

'Stanley? He's the owner of the Stagshaw site?' When Ridout nodded, Eric went on, 'I imagine he will be present in view of the serious nature of the charges you and the others are laying.'

'He's got other sites you know. Down south. I wondered whether he'd be too *busy* to put in an appearance,' Ridout sneered.

Eric doubted it. There would be too much riding on the claims for the owner of Stagshaw Waste Disposal.

'Right, well, the meeting is scheduled for next week. Stanley's lawyers will be there; you'll be representing the villagers and I'll be relying on you to state a case in the first instance. Not too much detail—just enough to introduce our files and written evidence. And I'll bring in Dr Armstrong—he's agreed to be retained by us to comment upon the medical implications of the files. But in particular I'll want you to bring in the history of the site, and the events that have shown a pattern of negligence and incompetence in the management of the Stagshaw site.'

Something rumbled deep in Ridout's throat. His eyes glittered. 'So you'll want me to talk about the dozens of complaints we've filed over the last five years. Disregarded; usually unanswered. About the dizziness we've all suffered occasionally when the wind is blowing south-east. About the sore eyes, the stomach upsets, the burning sensations on our top lips . . .'

'I'll want you to take a close look at this file,' Eric suggested, placing a manila folder in front of him. 'It contains details of these symptoms, and of the people named who have suffered, together with the rough diary of dates. It would be useful if you could check it out for inaccuracies, or anything we've missed.'

Ridout opened the file, his eyes hard. He read through it silently, lips moving slightly as he scanned the pages. He nodded. 'I'll keep it by me—it'd be better if I can talk to it, than just read it out at the meeting, hey?'

'That's right. And I'd better explain to you about the question of damages. You can show cattle deaths—'

'Five to date.'

'But the evidence, the connection between the deaths and the Stagshaw site?'

Ridout grunted in contempt. 'The vets were

unable to fix on a cause of death so we sent them to the Ministry lab to assess the level of poison.'

'What toxins did they find?'

Ridout grunted. 'It was a cock-up, or a cover up, I'm not sure which. It seems the scientists were unable to agree even on whether the tests should happen. But animals don't just die. And shortly after the fires.'

'You have details of the fires,' Eric prompted.

'That's right,' Ridout growled. 'Over the years there've been three fires at the site. Small enough, except for the first one in 1997 when there was a biggish outbreak and explosion and we got a sort of purple-red rain over the village. It drifted over here, to the farm as well. It was like a gas—we called in the police and they sealed off the village for a few hours. But that was all they said they could do. That was when I went on down to Stagshaw, to try to see Lon Stanley, but he wasn't there. And the manager wasn't admitting anything. But I did get to talk to one of the workers there—Ken Gordon his name was. He told me he was disgusted with the way things were run there. He told me their firefighting procedures were a joke and their decontaminating systems useless. He told me he nearly got injured himself when a drum of chemicals burst when he was trying to wash it.'

'His name doesn't appear in our witness

list,' Eric frowned.

Ridout scowled. 'He was killed last winter. That heavy snow we had: he skidded in his car, collided with a roadgritting machine. Killed outright. But I can testify to what he said—'

Eric shook his head. 'You could only testify that he had spoken to you. It would be treated as mere hearsay as to its truth. No, we can't rely on that. And then there's Sam . . .'

Ridout's jaw clenched angrily. He glared at his mug of coffee, and Eric was aware of the effort it took the man to control his feelings. 'I been to see him, just yesterday. There's no change. He's just wasting away. And it's that bloody dump that's been killing him. He was a strong lad, you know. My only son. He was to take over this farm when I'm gone—carry on a tradition, like. Our family's been here for generations. And it's a healthy life, working on the land. Up on the fells, out in the open . . . But for him, it's been a death sentence. That bloody site at Stagshaw, it's that what's been killing him.'

Carefully, Eric explained, 'There might be some difficulty about proving that—if Sam does die. What the Stagshaw people are going to argue, and perhaps show, is that as the second largest waste disposal company in the country they have a sound reputation for safety. They are claiming that even though the facility at Stagshaw includes two large chemical storage units that are really uncovered wells

24

over a hundred years old, and six concrete lined consolidation pits open to the elements, they have had the site regularly inspected by government officials, in accordance with the grant of their licences. Moreover, the local management are insisting they do not cut corners in order to make their facility better able to resist competition, as one of our witnesses suggest.'

'Colonel Martin,' Ridout growled. 'He made a study of it.'

'Stagshaw refute his figures. And they have the advantage of us there.'

'How about the fact that the county allowed storage there without planning permission?' Ridout demanded aggressively.

'That pre-dated the take over of the site by Stanley,' Eric explained. 'And although the site was allowed to continue its operations when the oversight was discovered—which seems mind-boggling to me—new regulations had been brought in subsequently after an environmental risk audit was carried out. Stagshaw's licence was renewed only last year. I don't think we'll get much leeway out of that issue. They'll say it's just history, and out of their control.'

Eddie Ridout was silent for a little while. He flicked at the file in front of him with a gnarled, broken-nailed finger. 'Are you telling me we don't have a chance?'

Eric shook his head. 'No, I'm not saying

25

that. I'm simply stating the case they'll be presenting. It's up to our side to come up with provable, particular situations—'

'Like Sam.'

The words hung between them, flat, but shimmering with a dangerous fury.

Carefully, Eric said, 'What we need to do is to show Stagshaw that there is a case to answer. They won't want the issues to go to court—there would be too much bad publicity for them, and who knows what local authority or government worms might get turned up.'

'They should be taken to court!' Ridout hissed angrily.

Eric stared at the man silently for a little while. He could understand Ridout's feelings, the suppressed anger, the fury at the violence done to his life, the frustration at being unable to take the direct action that would come naturally to him. He shook his head. 'A court action should be a last resort, Mr Ridout. Let's try to get what we want without it. A hearing in court could result in delays, enormous expense—and at the end of it, maybe the wrong result. We must try to persuade Stagshaw that compensation is payable, that the site must be cleaned up or closed—though I doubt we'll get them to agree to the latter. We must force a settlement on them, get them to agree that—'

'*Settlement*,' Ridout sneered. 'Those bastards, they've poisoned the village, they've

26

given my son a poisoned life. Settlement? I'd as soon see them hang.'

'I know how you feel, Mr Ridout,' Eric said slowly. 'But we have to deal in realities. The art of the possible. We must try to stop them, and make them pay for what they've done. But—and I say it as a lawyer—the courtroom should be seen as a last resort.'

Eddie Ridout leaned back in his chair and folded his arms. He stared hard at Eric, and his eyes were like slivers of ice, his mouth twisted, his jaw hard. 'Last resort? No Mr Ward. For me the last resort is my getting these hands around Stanley's throat. He sits down there in London, and he swans around in his big cars, and he makes his millions, and he thinks he can get away with everything just by bringing in some smart-arse lawyers to talk his way out of trouble. But in the end, it's an eye for an eye, Mr Ward. You talk to me of settlement. But for me, there's one final way to settle this. And I could do it, too. Mr Lon Stanley?' He held out his hands, stained, calloused, powerful. 'The way I feel, I could snap his bloody back!'

2

The Quayside was busy when Eric arrived in Newcastle: traffic thundered over the Tyne bridge above him as he cruised around seeking a parking place. Eventually he was forced to park the Celica near the *Blue Moon* restaurant but he guessed he wouldn't be too long in the office anyway. The reason for the crowded waterfront was apparent when he walked around to his office: several busloads of gawking tourists come to see the wonder of the new Millennium Bridge between Newcastle and the Gateshead bank.

He entered the side door to the old Exchange building and made his way up the stairs to his office. His was not a fashionable address although it was conveniently situated for the Law Courts on the banks of the river, now overlooking the Millennium bridge. But neither was his practice a fashionable one: he was aware that even his secretary Susie Cartwright rarely approved of his clientele, and felt he could do better. She had told him so several times: practical, loyal, protective but always outspoken, she sometimes sniffed contemptuously when she showed in a client she did not approve of. Eric tended to ignore her attitude, because he valued her services and liked her for her forthrightness.

She had been with him for two years now: tall, slim, forty and widowed. He suspected she did not need the money—not that he paid her a great deal—but she enjoyed the work, if not all the clients.

'You've got a Mr Paulson coming in.' She checked her watch. 'About half an hour. It'll give you time to deal with some files I left on your desk, Mr Ward. Legal Aid claims. And the Board will be sending someone next week, to check you out.'

Eric winced. That was something he could do without—the regular need to convince the Legal Aid Board that he ran an efficient practice with clients usually requiring legal aid. He walked into his office, leaving the door open. He sat down behind his desk and riffled through the files. He was aware she was watching him, standing in the open doorway.

'Was there something else?' he asked.

She hesitated; a hand stole up to touch her short, greying hair in a nervous gesture. 'You . . . have you heard anything about Mr Leonard Channing recently?'

Eric had never got on well with Channing— they had been deadly rivals while Eric had served on the board of the merchant bankers, Martin and Channing. But all that was over now. Eric had resigned from the board, and Channing had suffered a heart attack after his involvement in the call girl scandal six months ago. 'I don't believe he still retains the chairmanship of the merchant bank,' Eric said slowly. 'Since the heart attack, I think he's taken a back seat. I don't even know whether he's still on the board.'

'You're no longer involved with them at all?' she asked.

He stared at her, curiously. He shook his head. 'No, I resigned some time ago.'

'When exactly, if I may ask?'

Eric grunted and shrugged. 'I can't imagine why you should be interested, but it's about six months ago. Around the time Leonard Channing was hospitalised. But what's this all about?'

Susan Cartwright hesitated. She seemed vaguely troubled. She fluttered her hand in an uncharacteristically helpless gesture. 'There's been an article in the local newspaper at the weekend. I don't know whether you've seen it.'

Eric shook his head. 'I didn't read the weekend press. An article? About what?'

She gnawed slightly at her lower lip. 'It doesn't exactly name names. But it's about a boat called the *Princess Eugenie*. When you were still active on the board of Martin and Channing, and I was filing your board papers, I seem to remember coming across the name. Weren't Martin and Channing somehow involved with that ship?'

Eric leaned back in his chair, frowning. From the river he heard the mournful hooting of a tug, proceeding up from Wallsend. He stared blankly at his secretary, thinking back. Then he nodded. 'Yes . . . the *Princess Eugenie*. I wasn't involved with the business, although I recall seeing it in the board papers. It was an insurance matter, in the end. It was all settled, late last year.' He raised an interrogative eyebrow. 'So what's your interest in it now?'

'I told you, Mr Ward. There was this piece

in the paper at the weekend. I cut it out. I think you'd better read it.'

She turned away, rummaged in her desk and then returned, with a newspaper cutting in her hand. 'It's probably nothing,' she suggested, 'but I thought you might be interested to see it. I mean, it doesn't mention Mr Channing, or the bank itself, but I just thought . . .' Her words died away as he took the cutting from her. She turned, closed the door quietly behind her. Eric stared at the neatly trimmed newspaper article.

MYSTERY WRECK IN MEDITERRANEAN

The loss of the *Princess Eugenie* was always something of a mystery. Not quite the *Marie Celeste,* but curious enough nevertheless. The ship was built in 1952 and, it seems, insured against the usual perils of the sea. But it was lost in the Mediterranean, in good weather. No satisfactory explanation was ever made for the reason behind the sinking, though it was suggested—and claimed by the shipowners—that the *Princess Eugenie* had been holed by a submarine. The underwriters, on the other hand, claimed that the holing was due to the poor condition of the ship, arguing that it was not in fact seaworthy. In the ensuing action, it was held that the burden of proof as to what had caused the sinking lay upon the shipowners. Since there was a real doubt as to the reason for the sinking, the owners had not discharged the burden of proof. So their action against the underwriters failed, and no insurance payout was made in respect of the loss of the ship itself.

But it was another matter as far as the cargo was concerned. And now further facts are coming to light. Questions are being asked about certain letters of credit and a bill of lading. There are rumours that there had been a fire on board the *Princess Eugenie*. And certain parties are now disputing whether all was what it seemed to be, the day the *Princess Eugenie* disappeared. In the firing line are a prominent lawyer, and a well-known firm of merchant bankers in the City. So far, ranks have been closed, and everyone concerned is being very tight-lipped. But in a matter of weeks we may see more about the *Princess Eugenie* as divers finally manage to reach the wreck—and the mystery of her sinking, and of the cargo she carried, are finally revealed.

Eric rose slowly, walked across to the door. He opened it and stepped into the anteroom. Susan Cartwright looked up as he handed her the cutting. 'Not me,' he said lightly. 'I could never be described as a *prominent lawyer* now, could I?'

She sighed in mock regret and disappointment. 'Just as I thought I might be working for a personality.'

He hesitated. 'On the other hand, do you still have the old board minutes on file?' When she nodded, he went on, 'I think you'd better dig them out. No hurry about it. But I'd better take a look to refresh my memory, see what the issues were at the time. As far as I recall, I wasn't actually involved . . .'

'What about Mr Channing?' she asked.

Eric grinned wryly. 'Leonard Channing was always involved—in everything!'

He returned to his desk, picked up the files Susie had left for him, but he was unable to concentrate on them. The *Princess Eugenie.* It raised no great alarm bells in his memory, but he remembered vaguely that at the time of the sinking there had been a considerable flurry in the offices of Martin and Channing. The bank had certainly been involved in insurance matters concerning the ship. They had not been his direct responsibility but there was something fluttering at the back of his mind, an errant butterfly of recollection. He shook his head. Maybe if he took another look at the old files it would come back. It was of no great importance. He was well out of the whole business of Martin and Channing. He had only joined the board to look after Anne's interests and he had gained little pleasure from the involvement, or from the battles he had had over the years with the chairman Leonard Channing. And yet, there was something . . . a niggle at his memory He dismissed it.

He worked on the files before him for the next twenty minutes, until Susie buzzed him. 'Mr Paulson is here, Mr Ward.' There was a certain cool disdain in her tone which led him to believe that Mr Paulson was going to be a client of whom she did not approve.

When Paulson entered the room, Eric understood.

The Quayside practice relied to a large extent upon the experiences Eric had built up over the years, when he was still in the police force. He had been a good copper and a straight one, and possibly he might still have been there even now, because he enjoyed the job, if it hadn't been for glaucoma. He could still remember the day he had gone in to see the police surgeon, George Knox, to be told that staying on with the police was no longer an option. The scratching of the cat claws at the back of his eyes, the problem of tunnel vision—it had all been laid out for him. Medication could control it, but the stress of police life would only make things worse. So he had left the force, taken a law degree, entered articles, become a solicitor. But he was still drawn to the low life on Tyneside: the ranks of the underprivileged, the hopeless, the

34

downtrodden, the disregarded. It was something Anne and her county set friends could never understand, when by lifting a telephone, talking to the right people, accepting appropriate offers he could have moved away from the river, obtained spacious offices further up in the city, become a *prominent lawyer.*

But it wasn't what he wanted. And it was why men like Paulson came to his office.

He was about five feet eight, lean, round-shouldered with a hunted look about his whole body. He was in his mid-thirties, Eric guessed; his hair curled to his collar, lank and greasy and he was shabbily dressed in a worn suit that had seen better days, with scuffed shoes that seemed too large for him as he shuffled into the room with a light, slapping sound. His pale cheeks were gaunt, hollowed unhealthily and his deepset eyes were of the searching kind, restless, flicking glances everywhere, as though convinced there were riches to be found if one moved fast enough. He sat uneasily on the edge of the chair, almost as though ready to spring to flight at the sound of a wrong word. And yet there was a certain cunning in his glance, a confidence that suggested he knew his way in the world, recognised it for its foibles and weaknesses and evils. Eric disliked him on sight. But that was no reason to refuse to listen to him.

'Mr Paulson.'

'That's me. Joseph Paulson. My friends call me Joe,' he leered. 'That is, they would, if I had any. But I'm a lone night owl, you know? I go my own way, do my own thing. And that don't give rise to . . . acquaintanceships.'

Eric believed him. 'And what can I do for you, Mr Paulson?'

The little man smiled; he had surprisingly white teeth, and their irregularity confirmed that they were his own. He drummed his skinny fingers on the arms of the chair. 'I got arrested last night.'

'I see.' There was a short pause. 'You'd better tell me about it.'

Joe Paulson seemed not to hear him. He was staring at the files on Eric's desk, and smiling a secret smile. After a few moments, as Eric grew restless, his glance slid up to the window overlooking the river, and the far Gateshead bank. 'Different place, this, for a lawyer. All the fat cats, they got posh offices up the hill, or along towards the bank, there. You know Northumberland Square, in North Shields?'

Eric nodded.

'That's where a lot of lawyers have their practices. Arrogant, wasteful, careless lot. I thought about being a lawyer once. Changed my mind. Took a degree in Psychology. Newcastle University. That surprise you, Mr Ward?'

Eric was surprised, but was not prepared to

admit it.

'It's about appearances, isn't it?' Paulson continued. 'You see me, and you make assumptions. Like what I'm worth, or what I do. But you could be wrong, as you well know. Same way, people make assumptions about you, going by appearances. Squalid little office down on the Quayside, when he's got a rich wife and could be lording it among the Northumberland gentry . . .'

Edgily, somewhat ruffled, Eric suggested, 'Perhaps we could get down to what this visit is about.'

Joe Paulson giggled. 'It's about appearances, I guess. I'm a man who doesn't go by appearances. They are so often deceptive. The rich and famous, the great and the good—how did they get there? And when they got there, how did they behave? You can learn a lot from the trashcans of Northumberland Square, Mr Ward. But not from yours, not from yours. It's one of the reasons I came to you, in my hour of need.'

Slowly, Eric said, 'I'm not quite sure what you're talking about.'

'I'm talking about security,' Paulson explained eagerly, in a sudden rush of enthusiasm. 'Lawyers, like doctors, have secrets to protect. They're bound by their own form of Hippocratic oath, aren't they? The doctrine of client privilege means a lawyer is duty bound to keep his client's secrets for him, not to divulge what he might have heard in his professional relationship. Isn't that the way it goes?'

'Of course,' Eric replied stiffly, 'But—'

'But the fact is, they don't!' Paulson asserted. 'They are careless with what they have in their hands. And while their negligence is reprehensible, it's as well they are negligent— they, and others. Because if they were more careful the rich and the famous, the great and the good, the fat businessman, and the pompous clergyman, their secrets would never come out, the lies, the evasions, the scandals, they would all remain buried. And that's just not in the public interest, is it?'

Eric's irritation was increasing. 'I'm sorry, Mr Paulson, but I'm not at all clear what you want. Can we get to the point?'

'The point, Mr Ward, is that I got arrested last night.'

'So you told me. But what did you get arrested for?'

The cunning smile returned, white teeth gleaming, sparkling with malice. 'For doing what I've done for years. Working for the public good, supporting their right to know!'

There was a short silence. Eric frowned. He had begin to realise that the man in front of him was not going to be rushed: he had an audience, he was going to unfold his story and his needs in his own time. It would be an exercise in self-justification, Eric knew. It was often the case: justification came before admission of culpability. Perhaps it was the need to be liked, or understood. Something of the kind was driving Joe Paulson.

'You remember the business about Lord Whitley a few years back? The rent boys in that house in Gosforth?'

'I remember vaguely,' Eric admitted.

'Scandalous, wasn't it?' Paulson grinned. 'And the explosion at Corsenside Works? That Roman Catholic priest and the nun from Hexham? The Army procurement contracts, and the fiddles involved up at Otterburn? Hey, I could give you a long list going back years—the Wooler operations, the dentist who couldn't stay out of his female patients's knickers, that love nest set up in Ogle by that pop star, that incest business over at the Vale of Breamish—the list can go on and on. I got it all filed, you know. In my Pandoras . . . that's what I call them, my treasure houses. There's three of them,' he added, with a hint of pride in his voice. 'Of course, there's riches there that I haven't tapped yet, I mean, you have to wait until a boil is ripe before you burst it, isn't that right, Mr Ward?'

'Are you suggesting—'

'Me. Joe Paulson. It was all me.' The little man leaned forward hungrily, as though eager for the drug of admiration. 'I came to you, because you're not like most of the other lawyers on Tyneside. You understand the need

39

for security. Nothing comes out of your office. But with the others, all it needs is a nocturnal instinct, a nose for the business, and the ability to root out of a pile of rubbish the kind of information that can bring down a cabinet minister or a bishop of the church!' He flashed his teeth in triumph. 'It's the lawyers who are the worst, in my view, though hotels, hospitals, banks, local government offices, you name it, they all do it. They don't shred the information, they don't dispose of documents efficiently, they just dump things without thinking—and then they're surprised when the shit hits the fan! And now they're trying to say it's my fault! Hey—it's a joke, right?'

Eric was beginning to see the light. 'You were arrested yesterday for theft.'

'Can you steal rubbish?' Joe Paulson spread his light-fingered hands wide in appeal. 'Can you steal something that someone's already thrown away? If this guy decides he doesn't want his office or his house cluttered, and dumps something in the dustbin, is it theft to acquire it and use it for the public good? In my book, it's not theft. It's giving the public what they want. That's what I do. And now the powers that be want to muzzle me.' He narrowed his mean eyes, staring suggestively at Eric. 'And don't get me wrong, when I use the word powers, I mean exactly what I say. Joe Paulson is not given to exaggeration. I'm talking big, important people here. I'm talking people who have something to lose. Judges, doctors, hospitals; surgeons, priests, businessmen; and politicians, don't talk to me about politicians! But I got respect, too, and I'll get support.' Pride seeped into his tone. 'These big noises, they're trying to muzzle me, but I've got power on my side too. Where do you think the media would be without me? Do you think it's these so-called investigative reporters who do the digging? Is it hell! They get the kudos; they get the by-lines; they get their MBEs and OBEs, but without me they'd get nothing! You name the paper, and I'll name my contact. No, it won't serve their best interests to see Joe Paulson reined in and closed down.'

Eric leaned back in his chair, observing the man in front of him. Paulson was animated, nervous with excitement as he related his reason for existing. Because that was what it was, Eric guessed: an obsessional activity. 'You've been raiding dustbins, waste bins—'

'That's right. Private and professional. And now they've arrested me. What'll they do?'

'Charge you with theft.'

'Can they do that?'

'I would think so. Even rubbish has a value in the eyes of the law. And you have no right to it. So, yes, I think they'll charge you, and the charge will probably stick.'

'What'll I get?'

'How many offences will you plead?' Eric

asked. Joe Paulson rolled his eyes. Eric shrugged. 'They'll fine you. Maximum, a few hundred, maybe. And they'll probably slap an injunction on you. So if you do it again, they'd be able to nail you for contempt of court.'

'It'll never happen.'

'Why?'

'Because you're going to help me, Mr Ward.'

'And how can I do that?' Eric asked carefully.

'By being my lawyer. By contacting my clients. By getting them to whip up media support. By putting pressure on certain people. By speaking up for me in court. This is a constitutional issue, Mr Ward. It's all about freedom of speech.'

'No. It's about petty theft,' Eric argued mildly.

'One of the greatest constitutional causes— freedom of speech in Parliament—arose from the sale of pornographic magazines to inmates of Fleet Prison.'

'Stockdale v Hansard, I know,' Eric replied, half smiling. 'But there are no great constitutional issues here. It's just stealing, Mr Paulson.'

'You help me, Mr Ward, and we can make it into a big issue. If you were different, I would tell you that you could make a big name for yourself out of this, but I know that isn't important to you. But I'm a little man and I got the big guns ranging against me, over nothing. And that the kind of thing that's brought you to take on office on the Quayside.'

He stood up, almost triumphantly. 'Ain't I right, Mr Ward? Have I sussed you out, correctly?'

Maybe taking a degree in Pyschology hadn't been a waste of time for Joe Paulson after all, Eric thought wryly, as his new client made his way out of the door.

3

The pain began again in the late afternoon.

It had been a heavy schedule that Susie Cartwright had arranged for him. It had not been intentional, she assured him, not an attempt to keep him busy and his mind off current anxieties. Even so, he had the feeling she was aware that he was somewhat preoccupied and withdrawn and was slightly worried about the matters he was not talking about, notably, the situation with Anne. Women had an instinct for such emotional matters, he knew: he had said nothing to Susie about his marital problems, but he knew she suspected something was awry.

So he was kept busy all week. There had been no call from Anne, during the evenings he spent at the flat—but then, he hadn't called her at Sedleigh Hall either. It was as though they were in the middle of a simmering truce. And during the days his diary was full: there was one whole day spent in judge's chambers with a defendant who had pleaded guilty to a football violence charge outside St James's Park, but who came up with facts that bore no relationship to those presented by the police. It took a long-drawn out discussion with the judge—a trial within a trial—so that the judge could come up with a specific version of facts he could bear in mind when sentencing. And Eric had clashed with local officers also over a forgery case where the evidence produced was, in his view, highly suspect, and saying so did not make him popular. He had the feeling that more and more he was seen as a turncoat, a traitor—an ex-copper who had gone over to the other side.

But long days in the magistrates court and the office, in the Crown Court listening to an incompetent barrister standing in at the last moment and incapable of mastering his brief, these were all par for the course, really—it was all part of the job, and could not account for the tension that was rising in him. It had to do with Anne, of course: he was not sleeping well as he inevitably spent early morning, restless hours dwelling on their crumbling relationship, the damage done to what had been a good marriage. Agonisingly, and to no good purpose he went over and over in his mind the possible causes, his own stupidity, her reticence about her behaviour of recent months, their joint failure to be open and honest with each other. The motivation for silence had seemed sound: a determination to spare the other unnecessary hurt. But somehow, it only seemed to be making matters worse, and as the time dragged on, the ability to speak out decayed, and further silence seemed the only solution.

And it brought back the pain at the back of his eyes. Pilocarpine assuaged it, but could not prevent its return at times of stress, or when he was tired, or emotionally drained.

So when he came out into the late afternoon sunlight of the Quayside, walking down the steps and away from the Law Courts, he had to sit down on a stone bench at the river's edge, rubbing his eyes as the slow tearing, scratching pain returned, feral claws, sandpaper against his optic nerve ends. People strolled past him, admiring the elegant sweep of the new bridge across the Tyne: it had taken the second largest crane in the world to bring it upriver after its construction, and now it was in place, not used yet as the finishing touches were put to it, but an attraction for afternoon strollers along the Quayside. He became aware of someone standing near the bridge; a man, fair, short-cropped hair and leather jacket, facing him, staring. Eric looked away. The sun sparkled on the dark waters of the Tyne but even the sunlight seemed too much for him eventually, and he rose, walked across the road and entered the cool dimness of the Prince of Wales bar.

He ordered a brandy and soda, and took the drink across to a seat in the darker area of the room. There were only two other people there, a man and woman, talking quietly at the far end of the room. From their body language he guessed it was an assignation, rather than a business meeting. Eric sipped his drink, leaned his head back against the cool imitation leather of the bench seat, and closed his eyes. There were intermittent flashes of light behind his lids, a redness, a painful glow that grew and diminished, but the pain was receding, slowly. He stayed like that for several minutes, waiting for relief.

'Are you all right?'

Eric opened his eyes. The tall man standing in front of him was in his early thirties. It was the man he had seen watching him, near the bridge. His hair was fair and cropped short; his eyes a pale, earnest blue; his features could only be described as craggy, a broken nose above a firm mouth. He was dressed in a leather jacket, open-necked shirt and jeans. He had an air of confidence about him: the breadth of his shoulders and the narrowness of his waist suggested to Eric that the man would spend more than a little time in the gym, working out. He was holding a glass of lager; his hands were strong, and his bearing upright, almost military

Eric shrugged. 'I'm fine.'

'I saw you on the seat. Out on the Quayside. You looked a bit groggy.'

'It's passed. A drink helps.' Eric was reluctant to continue the conversation but the stranger was already pulling a chair out from under the table, sitting down opposite Eric. 'You're Eric Ward, aren't you? I saw you in court. Your secretary told me you'd be there. I was going to try to have a word as you left court, but when you came out and sat on the bench, I thought maybe you wouldn't appreciate company.'

He still didn't appreciate company. But said nothing.

'My name's Karl Preece.'

He said it as though he expected Eric to recognise it. There were some men like that, Eric thought sourly: they expected everyone else to identify with their own little world, and admire the part they played in it.

'If it's a matter of business,' Eric said slowly, 'I'd rather you made an appointment to see me in the office.'

Preece laughed softly. 'Easier said than done. I've tried a couple of times but you were out.'

'My secretary wants me to prepare for my old age. But with the way she works me, I might never make it.'

'I thought all lawyers made a bomb,

47

financially.'

'There are lawyers, and lawyers.'

'Some who enter corporate and commercial fields,' Preece suggested, 'and have huge expense accounts—and others who work on the Quayside. I guess you'll be one of those who started with nothing, and still have most of it left.'

Eric was silent for a little while, feeling the slow smouldering of irritation. He was unwilling to admit that Preece was perhaps striking too close to home. He sipped his drink. 'What is it you want, Mr Preece? Free legal consultation?'

'Hell, no,' Preece replied, grinning. 'I'm a newspaperman. I just wanted a chat. Off the record so to speak.'

Eric observed him quietly for a moment, then said, 'I'm involved in no high profile cases that could possibly draw the attention of the Press.'

'You'd be surprised, Mr Ward. The courts can be the life blood of the newspapers—and small stories can suddenly grow very, very big. But it's not any case you're involved in at the moment—I just wanted a chat, about general things.'

'Then you're wasting your time. I'm no philosopher,' Eric replied, irritation now appearing in his tone. 'So, really, if you don't mind—'

'Well, when I say *general*, I guess I really

mean background. But to something specific.'

'You're confusing me.'

'Something specific—like the *Princess Eugenie*.'

Karl Preece rose abruptly and walked away towards the bar. Eric sat still, frowning. He was sorely tempted to finish his drink quickly, and escape back to the office, tidy up his outstanding files and make his way back to the flat for an early evening. But curiosity held him in his seat. When Preece returned he was carrying a glass of brandy and soda. He placed it in front of Eric. 'Don't let it be said that the Press don't pay their way—'

Eric eyed the drink sourly. 'A small enough price.'

'The street says you're one of an unusual kind: a straight lawyer.' Preece grinned again. 'So I wouldn't even attempt a larger bribe.'

'The *Princess Eugenie* . . .' Eric paused, wondering. 'There was an article, in the newspapers last weekend.'

'I wrote it.' Preece leaned back in his chair, slipped out of his jacket. His arms were lean, well-muscled. He looked more like an athlete than a reporter. 'And I'm following up on it. Which is why I thought it would be useful to talk to you. How's Leonard Channing?'

The question caught Eric by surprise. He stayed on guard. 'Not well, the last time I saw him.' When Preece made no further comment, Eric went on, 'But what makes you think I

49

have any information that you might find useful in your . . . researches?'

Preece sighed, and stared at his drink thoughtfully. 'Well, I'll tell you. There've been rumours flying around for a while, and I've picked up various pieces of information here and there. But my sources have sort of dried up, leaving me with a number of unanswered questions. So I've sort of got to get back to the start, if you know what I mean.'

Eric shook his head. 'I don't see how I can help you.'

'Well, some general information really. You yourself were on the board of Martin and Channing when they got involved in the underwriting of the marine insurance.'

'I was, yes. I no longer am on the board, of course.'

'Of course.' Preece smiled slyly. 'Gossip was you and the chairman Leonard Channing never really got on too well.' When Eric made no reply, he went on, 'And now Channing himself has had a heart attack, and can't be interviewed—or chooses not to be available— and I'm struggling to get to grips with the story.'

'What story?' Eric asked.

'Ah, well, there we are.' Preece hunched himself forward in his chair, adopting an air of confidentiality that in no manner fooled Eric. 'So far, we have the story of the mysterious disappearance of the *Princess Eugenie* in the

50

Mediterranean. The one side say that the ship was perfectly seaworthy, but was holed by a submarine. The other side say she was a rustbucket that should have been scuttled years ago.'

'Which is what you talked about in your article. But since I was never involved in that particular piece of business at the merchant bank, I don't see there's any information I can give you to help in the matter.'

'Ah, well, it's not really the story of the *sinking* as such that I'm interested in,' Preece confided. 'Submarine or accident or unseaworthiness, that'll all come out in due course, I've no doubt. It's certain other matters I'm sort of looking into.'

'Such as?'

Preece was silent for a little while, thinking. Then he sniffed, looked about him with a conspiratorial air. 'I don't tend to go for these kind of mysteries of the sea, normally. Most of my work in the media is concerned with business. I write an investment column at the weekend, for one of the nationals. That's really where my main interests lie.'

'A shares tipster.'

'Sort of. I watch the markets; predict trends; offer advice. And that kind of work means that I get to know quite a lot of people in the business and finance world. People talk. And snippets of information suddenly emerge, often seemingly unrelated.'

51

'And you've heard something involving the *Princess Eugenie*?'

'You might say that,' Preece replied carefully. 'You ever heard of a company called Equitable and Marine?'

Eric shrugged. 'The name rings no bells.'

'That's funny,' Preece said in a casual tone. 'I'm told they had connections with Martin and Channing.'

'Not that I'm aware of. But the merchant bank had several areas of activity in which I had no involvement, before I left them. I was there really as a legal consultant, looking after the interests of Morcomb Estates.'

'Of course. Morcomb Estates. That's really your wife, isn't it?'

'You're well informed,' Eric said stiffly.

'I'm a newspaperman,' Preece replied as though that explained everything, but Eric was aware of a certain undercurrent in the man's tone that left him slightly edgy. 'You resigned from the board for personal reasons,' Preece continued. 'I presume you were replaced— someone else took over the brief, looking after the interests of Morcomb Estates.'

Eric made no reply; he felt it was none of Preece's business. And there was something about the man's manner that suggested he was holding something back.

'I understand the seat on the board, the seat you vacated, was taken by a Queen's Counsel. By the name of Sullivan.' Preece paused, but

Eric said nothing. 'So he's now looking after your wife's . . . interests.'

Eric kept a curb on his rising anger. He was overreacting; Preece could know nothing, wouldn't even be interested in Eric Ward's personal problems.

'Sullivan had a previous involvement with Morcomb Estates, I understand, in some Singapore business last year. Which fell through.'

'I thought we were discussing the *Princess Eugenie*,' Eric commented.

'Well, maybe we're not too far from that matter all the time.' Preece finished his lager, pushed the glass to one side and leaned forward, elbows on the table between them. 'When exactly did Jason Sullivan take the seat on the board of Martin and Channing?'

Eric shrugged. 'When I resigned.'

'Was he involved with the bank before that? I mean, did he have any dealings with Martin and Channing? Or for that matter, with Morcomb estates?'

'I wouldn't know. I'm not Jason Sullivan's keeper.' He was unable to keep the sharpness out of his tone. Preece noticed it; his eyebrows rose a trifle as he stared at Eric.

'Well,' the reporter continued, 'maybe I ought to put you in the picture regarding these . . . rumours I've been hearing. See if they strike any chords, ring any bells for you. The *Princess Eugenie*, she carried the usual marine insurance against perils of the sea. Some of that insurance cover was underwritten by Martin and Channing. And there's a lawsuit pending with regard to payments out—the dispute being the submarine or unseaworthiness arguments. But were you aware there was a second insurance company involved?'

'I was not.'

'So if I told you that Equitable and Marine had entered into a separate policy with the shipowners, covering the cargo carried by the ship . . .?'

'I wouldn't know about that.'

Preece smiled, almost as though he didn't believe what Eric was saying. 'It was denim, I understand, on the *Princess Eugenie*, denim carried c.i.f. on Limassol terms. Letters of credit were issued providing that shipment was to be made in certain parcels on certain dates. Policies were issued—by Equitable and Marine—and a bill of lading drawn up complying with the letters of credit. The denim was loaded. The *Princess Eugenie* left port. Then, mysteriously, she went down.'

'You seem to have the facts, I've nothing to add to them. You know more than I do about it all, seems to me.'

'Maybe so, maybe so,' Preece replied smugly. 'Another drink?'

'No, thanks. You've corrupted me enough. One brandy and soda is a big enough investment for a return that's clearly going to be very small.'

Preece grunted. 'I have all the facts. Maybe. But as I said, there's rumours, too. I've not been able to get a statement out of Equitable and Marine, but certain . . . information has been sneaking in to my office that all is not what it seems.'

'How do you mean?'

'The denim.'

'What about it?'

'I've heard that it didn't actually go down with the *Princess Eugenie*. The scuttlebutt is that some of the cargo has turned up in Turkey, but I've not been able to verify that. However, it's being suggested that maybe the cargo of denim was transhipped—before the unfortunate vessel set out on its final voyage.'

Eric was silent. He had no idea whether Preece had any evidence to back up his statement, but Eric could appreciate the implications, if Preece's information was sound. The circumstances surrounding the sinking of the *Princess Eugenie* were themselves the subject of considerable discussion, with nothing yet resolved between the disputants as to insurance liability for loss of the vessel itself. But now there was a new dimension suggested: the possibility of fraud. The *Princess Eugenie* had been scheduled to carry a cargo of denim, insured by a separate company, Equitable and Marine. A claim would lie against the insurers for the loss of those goods. But if those goods had not actually been on the vessel when she went down, the contract was void and the question also arose—where were they?

'I can see from your expression that you recognise the little problem we have here,' Preece said slowly. 'Insurance cover on goods that maybe weren't actually on board. An insurance claim against that cover. We're maybe talking of conspiracy, fraud, and what else? You know a man died when the *Princess Eugenie* went down? And there's talk of a possible fire having broken out on board. So what have we got—arson, theft, fraud, murder, shipwreck?'

'Or plain moonshine,' Eric said dryly. 'How much of this is just speculation?'

Preece shrugged his broad shoulders. 'I'm speculating, that's for sure. But that's my business.'

'And what do you hope to get by talking to me about it?' Eric wondered.

'I'm not sure. Maybe you can help me fit into place some pieces of a jigsaw. Overlapping interests. Fraudulent opportunities. Just who's doing what to whom. I come across questions like this all the time in my business column. And since it seems to me you've been around, sort of involved at the fringes, at the edges of this whole *Princess Eugenie* thing—'

'I hardly think so. True, I was on the Martin and Channing board, and the bank did underwrite the marine insurance, but I was not personally involved in it, and as for the possible fraud, or other activities you mention, I don't see that—'

'Did you know that the company that insured the cargo, Equitable and Marine, are a Newcastle based insurance company?' Preece asked in an innocent tone. 'Grey Street, in fact. Finest street in Europe, some say.'

Eric hesitated. He had had enough of this conversation. Something told him he was on the edge of an issue he would not find pleasant. 'I know nothing at all about Equitable and Marine, but if you say they're a northern company I'll take your word for it. Now if you'll excuse me, I think we'd better call it a day—'

'So you don't know who the directors of Equitable and Marine are,' Preece pressed.

'I've no idea,' Eric said shortly, rising to his feet. He picked up his glass, finished the drink. 'Thanks for the hospitality; it's time I got back to my desk.'

'One of the non-executive directors, until recently, was Jason Sullivan QC,' Preece said quietly.

Eric stared at the reporter as the silence grew around them.

After a while, Preece leaned back in his chair, raised his arms and stretched, grunting as his shoulder muscles cracked. 'Sedentary job, that's the trouble. If I don't work out regularly, keeping fit and in shape . . .' He glanced up at Eric, staring at him. 'It's the sequence, you see. It puzzles me. Martin and Channing underwrites the sea perils for the *Princess Eugenie*; the ship sinks in mysterious circumstances; there's some doubt about the location of the cargo, insured by Equitable and Marine; Jason Sullivan was a director of Equitable and Marine and is now on the board of Martin and Channing . . . Just what does this merry-go-round mean? Just what the hell is going on?'

Eric's mouth was dry. 'Probably nothing.'

Preece held his head on one side, like an inquisitive blackbird. 'We gentlemen of the Press, we never think along those lines. Smoke and fire. I guess you yourself have never been caught up in this *Princess Eugenie* thing, but it's a bit of a coincidence, isn't it—you resigning from the board and Sullivan taking over. And what about Leonard Channing? What does he know about all this? And what the hell has Sullivan been up to? Has there been a conflict of interest? Has there been fraud? What happened to the cargo? You see my point, Mr Ward? Probably nothing, you say. But maybe . . .'

He stood up, shrugging. 'Well, I'll just have to keep digging. See you around.'

He turned, picking up his glass and walked back to the bar. Eric stood there for a moment, his mind churning. He could not pinpoint the source of his unease. Preece was talking of rumour, unproven facts, coincidences . . . But Eric was still uneasy. He tried thinking back, pinpointing a date when exactly Jason Sullivan had first been in contact with Martin and Channing. Or, more to the issue from Eric's point of view, when had Sullivan first become friendly with Anne?

He took a deep breath and began to walk towards the door. It was probably that Preece was weaving a web of fantasy, all based on supposition, and rumour . . . not hard information.

At the door Eric stopped, thinking for a moment. Hard information. He turned, and went back to the bar. He stood beside Preece: the man was perhaps three inches taller than Eric, who stood at six feet. 'So,' the reporter said softly,' you had second thoughts about what you know, Mr Ward?'

'No.' Eric hesitated. 'But you've been asking me some questions—maybe you're prepared to let me ask you a few.'

Preece chuckled. 'Ask away.'

'The information you've been talking about. Where did it come from?'

'We don't divulge our sources, you must know that.'

'So it's just rumour, chat . . . no documentary evidence of any kind?'

Preece's eyes narrowed. 'I didn't say that.'

'But if you had documentary evidence, you

59

wouldn't have been asking me for help.'

'Maybe I've got *some* documentary evidence, that needs filling in,' Preece replied carefully. 'What's this about?'

'I just wonder whether the . . . information you received came from a client of mine.'

'And who would that be?'

Eric looked him straight in the eye. 'A man called Joe Paulson.'

There was a brief silence. Something moved, deep in Karl Preece's pale blue eyes: it could have been uncertainty, disbelief, or even amusement. Then he laughed, the sound barrelling out of his broad chest. 'You must be joking! That little scumbag? I wouldn't touch anything from him with a fumigated bargepole!'

'Mr Paulson tells me he has dealings with a number of newspapers,' Eric said in a level tone.

'Joe Paulson is a fantasist,' Preece sneered. 'Sure, he gets in touch from time to time, with me, with some other guys on the paper, with the desk editors, but I tell you he's a nut case. There's no way we'd give him house room. We're investigative reporters—we don't rely on the kind of trash and scuttlebutt he hawks around.'

'He tells me he has links with a number of editors. He wants me to talk to them, get support from them. He sees himself as acting in the public interest—'

'In his dreams!' Preece scoffed. 'He's a little man who grubs around in dustbins in back alleys, picking up the kind of stuff that the tabloids like to print. But it's all strictly small time stuff, salacious, dirt-grubbing of the worst kind. Editor support? He can forget it. We don't need him, and we don't use him. You'll get the same story from anyone in the business. Why should we use Paulson, when we have better, more reliable sources?'

Mildly, Eric said, 'But he tells me the information he gets is often original documentation, thrown out by accident, or through negligence.'

Preece stared at him, in open disbelief. 'You've taken him on as a client, you say? My guess is, you're the only lawyer on Tyneside who would! I tell you, Mr Ward, it doesn't say much for your practice, if you have to take on the likes of Joe Paulson. I know that lawyers don't think much about newsmen; and maybe we don't rate lawyers very highly either. But I tell you this. You've taken on Joe Paulson, but I don't know a single reputable reporter who'd have anything to do with that little scumbag.'

Or perhaps who would openly admit to it, Eric thought.

CHAPTER TWO

1

A year on Tyneside and Charlie Spate still hadn't settled into the job.

It wasn't that he disliked the area: it lacked the sprawl of London but produced many of the same problems: a riverside that spawned opportunities for drugs smuggling; rundown housing estates that were breeding grounds for the kind of mindless thuggery that led eventually to gang warfare; a culture that saw the police and any kind of authority as inimical; and just outside the city limits a wealthy upper crust that derided the attempts of the police to impose order out of chaos.

It wasn't the area—in fact, it held a certain appeal for him. It was more probably his hormones. They'd given him problems before, when he was working in the Met. The brass had never pinned anything on him, but the rumours and suspicions were enough to make them suggest it would be better for his career, and everyone else concerned, if he moved on. He'd become an embarrassment. Favours from prostitutes, they hinted, but didn't come up with the evidence.

And there were more than enough prostitutes along the Tyne, in Shields, in

Sunderland, in Middlesbrough, around the clubs and drinking dens in Newcastle. And he'd heard the middle class enclaves in the Northumberland villages could also be happy hunting grounds for a man in mufti with an urge. Bored, lonely wives whose husbands were too busy making money to pay them the attention they thought they deserved.

But he was taking no more chances of that kind, not Charlie Spate. He'd managed to retain his DCI rank, coming north. He was averse to throwing it away for a brief release of sexual tension. Though he had to admit he had occasional dreams which involved Detective Constable Elaine Start. She had the kind of muscular legs that could clamp around a man like a nutcracker.

So to speak.

He sighed. The image disturbed him. He'd had enough of paperwork: a sub Post Office snatch; possession of firearms without a certificate; importation of obscene articles—they'd come in on a freighter on the Tyne and were still being 'checked out' by some of the junior officers. He'd heard their ribald laughter when he walked past the evidence room. He hadn't looked at the video tapes himself: his hormones were giving him enough trouble as it was. He pushed the papers aside and stood up. Time he went to see Connelly.

He walked out of the office and down the corridor. Someone was banging on the door of one of the cells protesting his innocence in a thick Glaswegian accent. A bold-eyed young woman passed him in the corridor, her arm gripped by a policewoman: he caught her careless, appraising glance and could guess what she'd be in for. He looked in at Connelly's room.

'He's not in?'

The fresh-faced young copper standing near the window shook his head. 'He's in the canteen. Gone for a cuppa.'

Charlie Spate winced. He'd got a cold, fish-eyed stare when he'd made his protest in the canteen about the quality of the beverages. *If that's a cup of tea, I'd like a cup of coffee. And if it's a cup of coffee, I'd like some tea.* His witticism hadn't been appreciated. But if that was where Connelly was, he'd join him there. It was likely that Connelly would be less outspoken in his annoyance, talking in the canteen. And Charlie had some sympathy for his point of view. You had to be hard with these bastards.

He turned back into the corridor. As he went past reception he paused: there was someone there he knew. Ex-policeman, turned solicitor. He went through the swing doors. 'Mr Ward. You're becoming a fixture down here among the dead men.'

The solicitor turned to look at him coolly. 'DCI Spate.'

Their relationship was an interesting one,

64

Charlie considered: they were like two, not unfriendly, dogs, circling each other, stiff-legged, curious, still not sure, careful, guarded, but perhaps with interests in common they were not prepared to admit to. He wondered whether Ward ever worried at the thought that he owed Charlie Spate, and whether he had sleepless nights over it.

'So what brings you to us today, Mr Ward?' Charlie asked brightly.

'My client has been here to make a statement.'

Charlie inspected the client with a wary eye. Slight, scruffy, hunch-shouldered, lank greasy hair. He was not impressed by the man's appearance, but he was rarely impressed by villains anyway. 'And you might be?'

'My name's Joe Paulson,' the man replied with, astonishingly, a hint of pride. 'You will have heard of me.'

'Ha, yes,' Charlie said. 'Mr Paulson. Your name is known here. The purveyor of information—dredged from the most unsalubrious of sources. How come you've never approached us with your little snippets? We're always on the lookout for a likely grass.'

'That's not the way it is,' Paulson replied, annoyed. 'I provide a public service. But I'm careful who I deal with.'

'That's a motto Mr Ward would be wise to adopt,' Charlie suggested. 'Public service, hey? Now if you were really serious about that, maybe you'd help us put some real villains behind bars—like the Mad Jacks of this world. Not messing about with trash you dig from dustbins.'

A cunning gleam had crept into Joe Paulson's eyes. He turned to Eric Ward. 'I think he's referring to Mr Tenby. But everyone knows he's gone straight, has Mad Jack Tenby.'

His tone suggested he knew something to the contrary. Spate doubted it: he'd heard that Paulson was low life, and more than a little weird. And if he did have something on Tenby, chances were he'd get stamped on as though he were a cockroach. Which was, no doubt, how some people looked at Paulson anyway. A black-backed, nocturnal, creeping thing that needed squashing.

Charlie turned away with a sniff of disgust, nodded to Ward. 'We must have a drink some time.'

Ward's expression suggested he did not find the prospect a pleasure.

Charlie headed off towards the canteen.

DI Connelly, thickset, gloomy, was sitting alone at the far end of the room, his hands cupped around a mug of warm liquid. Spate was disinclined to guess what it might be—though in his view, drinkable it would not be. He walked across the room; Connelly's head came up and he watched Charlie Spate's advance with a wary eye.

'Connelly.'

'Guv.'

'Mind if I sit down?'

'It's your canteen, as much as mine,' Connelly grunted. His tone lacked warmth.

'So how are things going?' Charlie Spate asked, dragging forward a chair and seating himself across the table from Connelly.

'Horses get used to certain pastures. When they're sent to graze elsewhere they get a bit miffed.'

'You're not enjoying the Shields assignment.'

Connelly's eyes were cold. 'I been there, done that. Chasing twockers around the estates; making lads pick up fish and chip paper blowing along Whitley Bay seafront; bouncing kids in and out of the magistrates courts; taking lip from young girls in the rat-run underpasses when you tell 'em to lay off the fizzy wine and Ecstasy; knocking on doors to talk to pink-slippered slags who swear their boyfriends were tucked up in bed with them that night when Safeways got turned over. Naw, like I said, I been there, and it's not the high life, guv.' He sipped his drink distastefully. 'It sort of lacks *purpose*.'

Twocking. Taking vehicles without consent. Drag races around the estates. Kids sniffing glue in the back lanes. Charlie knew all about it: like Connelly, he'd been there. It was unrewarding work. If the police car drove too fast to try to catch the villains there could be trouble—and even if the culprits were caught they were usually juveniles, got a slap over the wrist, and were back on the streets twocking again the next night.

'For what it's worth, I think it was a mistake, reassigning you. I gather this guy Blanchard is a hard case. And he did have a baseball bat.'

Connelly sighed. 'Well, you know how it is. The red mist comes up. Maybe I should have stopped a bit sooner. But you get carried away.' He eyed Spate thoughtfully. 'We all been in situations like that.'

'Right enough.' Charlie had put his own boot in often enough, though he had to admit never quite as much as Connelly seemed to have done with Blanchard. It had caused a lot of ripples when the police surgeon made his report: Connelly had been carpeted, pulled off the team, and told to cool off on an assignment, seconded to North Shields. 'Anyway, the Deputy Chief Constable has shoved the whole business onto me. So tell me about it.'

Connelly pushed aside the half empty mug and leaned back in his chair. He picked up the spoon, played with it idly between his fingers. The knuckles were still swollen. 'It was a drugs bust. We'd had a tip off a month or so back, from Middlesbrough, that a consignment of smack would be coming in to Tyneside, shipped into the Wear from Amsterdam, but

68

they were unable to trace the freighter that was bringing it in. They told us we could expect it slipping into Newcastle. So we made our own enquiries. When it all started coming together, the story was that Blanchard's pad would be on the receiving end, so we staked it out.'

'This Blanchard . . .'

'Danny Blanchard. A distributor. Not big time: he just does as he's told. But a hard man.' The sentiment reminded Connelly of his shoulder: he winced as he rotated it. 'We can't prove who's telling him what to do and when, and he's not the kind to open his mouth, even if he's facing a stretch. But we got interested in this event, because the story was that maybe Blanchard's controller was going to turn up. Anyway, we were certainly expecting someone else there that night: Blanchard's top contact. But he never showed. We waited, and when we realised the tip off was duff, we went in, took Blanchard, his team, and his stack. He'll go down for a few years this time—can't see his brief pulling something out of the hat for him, even if he is well paid by Mad Jack.'

'Tenby?' Charlie Spate asked softly. 'He's behind the business?'

Connelly eyed him coolly. He gave a non-committal shrug. 'It's my guess. Can't prove it, but I don't think leopards change their spots. Mad Jack may be presenting a respectable front these days, with his business interests,

69

and his posh dinner dates at big houses in Northumberland and Durham, but in my book he's still involved. He likes the buzz too much—and the money—not to keep his fingers stirring this particular pot. Mind you, the Deputy Chief is of another mind.'

'So I gather.' Charlie was aware of the problem. He had already had a run in with the Deputy Chief Constable over the issue: the DCC was convinced that Tenby was going straight, had put behind him the wild youth when he had battered his way to the top of the Tyneside gangs with a pick handle, earning himself the sobriquet of Mad Jack. The top brass view was that Mad Jack had reformed, now that he was playing footsie with the great and the good on Tyneside, but arriving new from the Met, Charlie Spate had picked up information here and there, recognised signs, and thought otherwise. He still did in spite of the views—and directives—of the Deputy Chief Constable. And it seemed Connelly was of the same opinion. Charlie Spate nodded. 'I'll pick up the files from you this afternoon.'

'Guv.' Connelly glared sourly at the spoon in his fingers. Slowly, he bent it until it almost formed a right angle. 'While I sniff around the Meadow Well estate to see if I can find anything on what Tinker Bell's up to.'

'Bell?'

Connelly raised an eyebrow. 'You haven't heard about Terry Bell? Tinker, we call him, because it gets up his nose. He doesn't like being compared with a fairy. He prefers the newspaper coverage. Batboy, they call him.' He snorted in disgust. 'He likes that. Gives him street cred.'

Slowly, Charlie Spate said, 'Didn't I hear something about—'

'The drugs bust. Aye, that's right. The little bugger was there. Hiding in the loft. Nearly got my hands on him, but he was away over the roof as usual. It's why they call him Batboy-flitting around the tiles. Here one moment, gone the next: now you see him, now you don't. The Great Escaper.'

'What's he got to do with the drugs scene?' Charlie wondered.

Connelly shook his head. 'I dunno. Not really his scene, unless he's graduating to bigger things now. I was surprised to see him there at Danny Blanchard's, but my guess is he was just using it as a pad to get his head down. I mean he's got to keep flitting, has Batboy, because the rope is getting shorter for him now.'

'How do you mean?' Charlie asked curiously.

Connelly shrugged. 'Terry Bell, the social workers will tell you, never had a chance. Meadow Well estate; an old man more interested in racing pigeons than fatherhood and separated from his wife; 'uncles' coming and going; mother down the pub most nights;

71

undersized, intelligent, scrawny, had to prove himself. So he did: twocking, thieving, burglary. Mostly small time stuff. But the last reckoning is sixty court appearances and thirty convictions. And a reputation for flitting out of custody like nobody's business. First time he escaped, they had to get the bloody fire brigade to get him down from the roof of the seafront marine laboratory. Since then, he's walked along girders fifty feet above the ground; hopped along the tiles of roofs and the corrugated iron of factories; crept in and out of sewage pipes and is reckoned to have done more twocking than anyone on Tyneside. I was talking to his social worker once: you know what they're like, the soft-boiled cretin said we shouldn't blame the young villain, we should put Terry Bell into his social context. He put it all down to dockyard layoffs, pit closures, decline of the Tyne fishing fleets, the development of Meadow Well as a drug-ridden ghetto, and thinks young Terry is just a victim of the environment. Custody should be a last resort; given time, the young bastard will grow out of it. Not a chance. And I tell you this, the day we get the little bugger inside for a long stretch, the crime rate will fall with a bump. We might even hit the targets the Home Office has stuck on us.'

'I presume he's done the usual run through the system.'

'System?' Connelly almost laughed, shaking

72

his head. 'He got put in a secure unit in Essex, first, then after that it was Newton Aycliffe Young People's Centre. He caused mayhem there: they had to get him down off the roof of the gym. Three thousand quid's worth of damage. And when he left there, the next step was Deerbolt Young Offenders. Didn't do much good: once he was out it was sixteen offences in six months. They might have taught him masonry, welding, bricklaying at Deerbolt but once he was back at Banbury Way on the Meadow Well, he was back to his old habits. It's about street cred, of course, as well as getting his hands on the readies. A break-in here, a robbery there. He's not big enough yet to get violent. It'll come, though. One of these days some poor old bugger will confront him in the middle of the night, and Batboy will put the boot in. It's just a matter of time.'

It was an old story, Charlie thought, nodding. He had seen boys like Terry Bell down south, on the run down estates. Sometimes he wondered whether it was not so much a record of crimes and misdemeanours, as an exhausted criminal justice system, failing at every turn to reform a miscreant youth. Carrots and sticks, short sharp shocks, the reform fashion of the day, the latest trend in youth justice, none of it seemed to have an impact on youngsters like Terry Bell, the Batboy.

'So you think he's upgrading himself, to

drug distribution?' Charlie asked.

Connelly swung his heavy head doubtfully. 'I don't know. Like I said, Tinker Bell is a sharp lad. He's a no-hoper and a thief, coming out of that group who flock down to play the gaming machines at Whitley Bay and do a bit of villainry on the way. But the drug scene is a bit heavy for him, I reckon. No, my guess is he was laying down his head. It might even be that Blanchard and the others didn't even know he was there at their pad. I wouldn't put it past the young bugger to have sneaked into that loft without their knowing. But until we get our hands on him, we won't know.'

'He'd be prepared to cop a plea, then?'

Connelly grinned. 'Hey, he can be angelic in front of the bench. Articulate, like. *I'm sick of it,* he says. *I want to change my life. I look around in the nick and see old men with grey hair and it makes me shiver.'* There was a hint of reluctant admiration in Connelly's voice. 'I tell you, the young bugger can charm the knickers off those middle-aged biddies on the magistrates bench. But he's running out of options. Next time, he knows, he'll get sent down for a stretch. He won't like that. And he knows a plea of mitigation will be of sod all use to him.'

'What's he wanted for at the moment?'

'Robbery. And burglary. But the drugs bust . . . my guess is he just happened to be there.' Connelly stroked his shoulder gingerly. 'But,

74

of course, I might be wrong. One thing I will suggest, though, guv. If he does turn up in your sights, keep a tight hold on him. It can be bloody embarrassing when a kid like that squirms out of cuffs and is gone over the top, up there with the rooks before you can say Jack Bloody Robinson. Or Jack Bloody Tenby, if you like.'

'I'll bear that in mind,' Charlie Spate said, doubting he would have any reason to chase the Batboy. Mad Jack Tenby, now, that was another matter.

He returned to his office, and sat there for a while, thinking. Then he wandered around headquarters, until he saw the person he was looking for.

'You got anything on tonight?'

Detective Constable Elaine Start looked up at him from her desk. She frowned. 'I don't mind a bit of overtime, sir.'

'You like to go dancing?'

'You asking?'

'I'm asking.'

'Then I'm dancing.' She leaned back in her chair. 'This isn't a date, of course.'

Charlie Spate smiled thinly. 'Not a date. And nothing to do with shaking a leg. More like pulling someone's tail.'

'And if I were to guess . . .'

She'd guess right. Mad Jack Tenby.

Charlie Spate picked Elaine Start up at her home in Kenton Bar. It was a modest, but respectable semi-detached house in a quiet cul-de-sac, on a housing estate near the main road. He was vaguely surprised, and perhaps he showed it when she came out of the house, where she had been watching for him at the window. She got into his car and glanced at him, shrugged. 'My parents used to live here. After they died, seemed no point in moving. I grew up here.'

'Geordie lass.'

'Something like that. So where we headed, sir? Shields?'

'That's about it. You've dressed for the part, I hope.'

'Unless it's ballroom stuff. I imagine it's a disco. So, usual gear; nothing too fancy.'

Something moved in his lower stomach. Charlie engaged gears and drove out of the cul-de-sac. He had had the sudden image of Elaine Start's backside, jiggling to a disco beat, and the thought, though pleasurable, disturbed him. He'd have to watch himself: the night was young and he didn't want to do anything stupid.

It was ten in the evening when they arrived at the nightclub. It was located down a side street. It was called Spring Heeled Jacks: heavy, hard-eyed, dinner-jacketed bouncers on guard just inside. They nodded politely to Charlie; he ignored them.

The room beyond was only half full, neon glinting off chrome bar stools; the darkened room next door with the flashing strobe lights reverberated to the beat of Motown music, but Charlie motioned Elaine to a table near the door. He went up to the bar and ordered a gin and tonic for his companion, and a beer for himself. As he waited, he looked around.

The woman perched on a high stool just feet away from him flashed him a smile. Her dark eyes were heavily made up; her long blonde hair carefully arranged to fall over her creamy shoulders; her lips were a brilliant scarlet. 'You got a light?' she asked, brandishing a cigarette. Her red dress was low cut, exposing the upper swell of her breast. Her English was heavily accented.

He shook his head, surprised at her amateurishness. 'Don't smoke. Where you from?' he asked, wondering about the accent. 'Romania?'

She smiled, trying to inject a desperate coyness into what was little more than a grimace. 'No, sir, I am from Russland.'

Spate looked at the barman, who gazed back at him expressionlessly. 'Flying them in from all over now,' Spate muttered, paying the barman. 'Has Jack Tenby come in yet this evening?'

'The boss? He usually looks in a bit later.

You wanting to see him? I could get a message. Tell him you're in.'

There was something in his tone, a certain contempt, that held a warning. Charlie smiled wryly. He'd already been recognised then—not as Charlie Spate, but as a copper. It was amazing the way they could sniff you out. He said as much to Elaine Start, after he returned with the drinks to their table.

She looked him up and down, critically. 'It's your manner,' she suggested.

'Are you about to speak out of turn?' he asked warily.

'If invited.'

'So go ahead.'

She took a sip of her drink, and wrinkled her nose, affecting to look him over carefully. 'Okay . . . you're about five ten, I think; got your own hair and teeth, lean, pretty fit, I guess. You could be an insurance salesman, but you have a mean mouth. You could be a college lecturer, but your eyes are too knowing. And you could even make out you're a family man, except you can't hide the arrogance that suggests otherwise. If you were married, you'd have been cut down to size a few times by your wife; but you're not, and it shows, and in a place like this you'll be picked out either as a hard case, or a copper. If you were a villain, they'd probably know you. If they don't, they'll guess you're fuzz.'

'You ever study psychology?' Charlie asked

78

sourly, not quite certain he had enjoyed her profiling him.

'Can't even spell it.' She turned her head, glanced towards the woman at the bar. '*She* hadn't sussed you, though. Looked like she was expecting to make a score with you.'

Charlie grunted. 'Russian. She'll be on the game. They're flooding in from the east, through Norway probably, to get here.'

'But you weren't interested in what she had to offer,' Elaine Start murmured. 'So what about me? We just going to sit here, or are we going to pretend to enjoy ourselves?'

Charlie looked over her shoulder, towards the disco. His reluctance was clear, and yet the thought of being close to her as she gyrated was tempting. He took a deep breath. The hell with it. He stood up, gestured towards the disco.

She smiled mockingly. 'You're so *masculine.*'

She walked in ahead of him. The short black dress showed off her legs to perfection. And when she turned under the flashing lights he became very aware of the view, the first swell of her magnificent bosom. She danced, and as the Motown beat got into his head he began to enjoy himself, almost forgetting this was business.

They stayed there for almost twenty minutes and the lights flashed around them, the beat of the music throbbed in his head, and adrenalin surged in his veins. He was barely able to make out her face as she twisted and turned but as they moved the back of his hands occasionally brushed against her breasts and he caught a glimpse of her eyes, mocking him. After a while the heat began to get to him, and his senses were confused. He jerked his head towards the bar.

When they went back to their table a bottle of champagne had been placed there, cooling in an ice bucket. 'Mr Spate, you *shouldn't* have,' Elaine Start cooed ironically

'I didn't,' he corrected her.

They sat down, and after a moment Charlie looked towards the barman. He was on the house phone. It wouldn't be long now, Charlie guessed.

Ten minutes later, with the champagne still untouched, the big man in the dark suit approached them. Broad in the chest, his grey hair cropped short and his craggy features at ease, confident, Jack Tenby loomed over them, affable, friendly. 'Mr Spate, good to see you again. And you Miss . . . er . . . Start isn't it? Always a pleasure to see you.'

The words were warm and welcoming but the eyes were as reptilian as Charlie remembered, calculating as he looked at them both. Tenby half turned, gesturing with a hint of pride. 'I should introduce you to my companion, Miss Fane. Carrie—meet our friends from Tyneside, DCI Charlie Spate and

DC Start. I doubt if they're on a date. '

The woman standing just behind Tenby came forward and extended her hand. She was perhaps thirty, Charlie guessed, maybe a little older. Her blonde hair was long, tied back carefully, allowing a few strands to fall over the side of her face. Her eyebrows were perfectly arched; her nose straight, her features regular, high cheekbones above a generous mouth. She was slim waisted but well endowed and the dress she wore accentuated her figure. She was a trophy for Mad Jack Tenby, of course—a woman thirty years younger than he.

'You from Russland too?' Charlie asked, offensively.

She took no offence. Her glance was cool as she said, 'Hell of a lot closer than that, Mr Spate. Local girl, me.'

Her accent marked her out as Sunderland, or Durham. She would have been a local beauty queen, Charlie guessed, before she took up with Mad Jack, and the dress and the bracelet she wore were expensive enough to suggest Tenby paid the bills. But she was no brainless blonde; her glance was shrewd, and he gained the impression it was not just the wisdom of the street.

'Carrie trained as a pharmacist,' Tenby explained, eyeing her appreciatively.

'That must be helpful for the business you're in,' Charlie murmured. 'Is that how you

81

two met? In a drugstore?'

Tenby recognised the implication behind the comment and didn't like it but kept himself in check. 'You've not tried the champagne. Best in the house.'

Charlie glanced at the bottle dismissively. 'I don't accept hospitality until I know what the price is likely to be.'

'Nothing to pay, Mr Spate,' Tenby assured him.

There was always something to pay, Charlie knew. He wasn't fooled by Mad Jack Tenby. The man professed to be a businessman, with a string of nightclubs, some legitimate businesses along the Tyne—printing, haulage, furniture manufacture—but Charlie Spate guessed that the excitement Tenby had used to experience when he was using muscle along the river had never entirely left him. Tenby may have built up a legitimate front for himself, but he would still be a chancer. He had fooled some of the senior officers on Tyneside, with his dinner parties, his friendship with politicians, his visits to stately homes whose owners were struggling to pay the bills and welcomed the occasional injection of cash from non-executive seats on the boards of Tenby's companies, but Charlie Spate knew a villain when he saw one, north or south of the Watford Gap.

'I thought I'd call in tonight,' Charlie explained, 'to let you know that I'll be treading on your toes again.'

Jack Tenby extracted a cigar from a silver case, walked away to the bar and got a light from the obsequious barman. He glanced at the Russian prostitute, meaningfully; she glared at him with real animosity, but after a few moments she slid off her stool and moved off towards the ladies room. Charlie guessed she'd be making herself scarce for a while now. He wondered about that.

When Tenby returned, he said, 'When I got a call that you was in here I did wonder whether it was just social. But when I saw Miss Start, of course, I knew it might be business.' He smiled at Elaine Start. 'Though I, of course, would never be able to keep my mind on business in your company, my dear. But then, I never could resist the weaker sex.'

'But it's men who are the weaker sex,' Elaine Start suggested sweetly.

Tenby puffed at his cigar. 'Now how do you make that out?'

'The weaker sex are the stronger sex because of the weakness of the stronger sex for the weaker sex.'

Carrie Fane gurgled her pleasure. Tenby waved his cigar. 'You must tell me the source of that quotation. It wouldn't be one of the films that you and I—'

'Never mind the bloody films,' Charlie Spate cut in, irritably. 'If you two want to talk Hollywood you can do it when I'm not around.

The thing is, Tenby, I'm just in tonight to keep an eye on things, see what you're up to these days—and to warn you that you shouldn't employ muscle like Danny Blanchard. Thugs like him, they're too addicted to mindless violence. I mean, what's the point in putting up a fight, particularly with a baseball bat, when you know you've been caught bang to rights?' He paused, thoughtfully. 'Of course, in your day it was a pickaxe handle, or so I hear. But that was a long time ago . . . long before your time, Miss Fane.'

She raised a cool eyebrow, then linked her arm through Tenby's, with a slow deliberation. 'I like older men. They have a history. It means they're real men.' There was a short silence. Tenby stood heavily, feet braced apart, staring down at Charlie Spate. At last, he said quietly, 'Danny Blanchard. I don't seem to be able to place the name.'

'He's one of your distributors,' Charlie explained patiently. 'He got picked up the other night. Blood everywhere. Mostly his. You really should have trained him better, Jack. It could have led to your having a quieter life yourself. You see, with Danny Blanchard putting up a fight he got hospitalised. And naturally, the top brass get worried in situations like that—police brutality and all that jazz—so they pulled the responsible officer off the case. Which means it's been swung on to me. And that's what I mean. You don't really want me on your case.'

'And why would that be?' Tenby asked coldly.

'Because I don't follow instructions easily. Because I don't go easy with villains. Because I don't believe it when a tiger starts wearing a dress suit and pretends he's really just a pussy cat. And because I know you're involved with what's been coming into the Tyne recently. Drugs. And from what I've seen tonight, prostitutes. However much you might deny it.'

Tenby was controlling himself with an effort. He laughed; it came out as a grunting sound, lacking real humour. He turned to the woman standing beside him. 'Carrie, Mr Spate here, he's got a kind of fixation about me. He's been proved wrong before; but he's a stubborn man who's never prepared to admit he's wrong. Even when I help him, as I did once before. Not that I can help him now—I can't, I don't even know what he's talking about.'

'Maybe Mr Spate suffers from monocular vision,' Carrie Fane murmured. Her voice was low in key and pitch; Charlie could imagine it whispering on a pillow.

'Optometrist as well as pharmacist,' Elaine Start commented.

The two women stared at each other with barely veiled animosity. It was entirely female and almost feral, and nothing to do with the fact they saw themselves on different sides of a fence.

Mad Jack Tenby grunted. 'Anyway, I can't stay here . . . gossiping. You got your job to do, Mr Spate, I know that, but don't waste your time coming around here on business. There's nothing for you in that line. If it's not just business . . .' His reptilian glance caressed Elaine Start. '. . . by all means, take advantage of all the house has to offer.'

He moved away, Carrie Fane leaning against him provocatively and throwing a cold smile back over her shoulder in Charlie's direction. Charlie was unsettled, a little angry. He felt he hadn't managed to drive home the point he wanted to make. Or maybe he resented Tenby's control and ease: the man felt he was safe with his big connections in the county. He reached for the champagne bottle, poured a glass for himself and Elaine.

'So we're living off the country now?' she enquired.

'Let's drink to his bad health,' Charlie suggested sourly.

Elaine Start sipped the drink, watching him carefully. 'And what exactly was the point of all this tonight?'

'Getting into his face,' Charlie muttered. 'Letting him know I'm around. Connelly might not have had the commitment to push Tenby hard; I do.'

'In spite of what the DCC thinks? This is beginning to sound like a vendetta. *Sir*.'

He was pouring himself another glass of

champagne. It was good stuff, he had to admit. And that Carrie Fane woman, she was good stuff too. He shook his head. She reminded him of some of the women he'd had dealings with down south. Most of them empty-headed. But Carrie Fane was something else, he considered: had the gut feeling that their paths would be crossing again before too long.

'You want to go back in there?' Charlie asked Elaine Start, nodding towards the disco.

She shook her head. 'I imagine you've done what you wanted to do, so the duty is over, isn't it?'

'Doesn't have to be all duty' he muttered.

'When I'm on the boards first thing in the morning, I like to get my beauty sleep.'

They left half of the bottle of champagne and went out to the car. It was a clear, sharp night with a bright crescent moon: it was something Charlie had noted about northern nights—it never really seemed to get dark. They got into the car but, instead of heading straight for the highway back to Newcastle, on a sudden impulse Charlie drove out along the headland. Elaine Start sat quietly beside him, saying nothing. He parked the car on top of the cliffs. He cut the engine, put his head back on the seat. He could hear the crashing of the waves on the beach below: along to his right he could make out the dark crumbling shape of the ancient abbey buildings, guarding the entrance to the Tyne at North Shields. He was in an odd, confused mood. He glanced at Elaine Start. She was staring straight ahead of her.

There was a short silence. Then she turned her face towards him: her eyes seemed to gleam in the darkness. 'I told you, sir. I need my beauty sleep.'

He reached for her, drew her towards him. She made no resistance. He kissed her, slowly. Her lips were cool, but unresponsive, controlled. In an odd way, it roused him: he felt as though he wanted to bring her to life sexually, impose himself upon her. Dark warnings flashed in his head: he had been here before, and it had cost him. But he was unable to resist the growing heat in his loins. He tried to kiss her again, but this time her hand was on his chest, firm; her head turned lightly aside.

'What's the matter?' he asked thickly. 'Don't you believe in pre-marital sex?'

'Why do you ask? You thinking of getting married?'

She always had a smart-arse answer. He released her, grinning suddenly. She didn't really need her beauty sleep—and he certainly wasn't thinking of getting married. But she knew how to save him from himself.

He started the car again, and drove her home to her semi-detached house at Kenton Bar.

*   *   *

Three hours later Carrie Fane let herself into the flat that Jack Tenby had bought for her in Gosforth. She switched on the light, and heard a small noise from the bedroom off the hall. She smiled to herself; a confident smile. She had guessed he would be here tonight. It had been almost a week, and he couldn't stay away even though he'd explained that it would be dangerous to come.

She wondered briefly what part the danger itself played in their relationship. She poured herself a whisky, and filled a second glass with the dark brown liquid. She slipped off her shoes, untied her long, blonde hair and carried the drinks through to the bedroom. The room was dimly lit: only the reading lamp beside the bed was on. He was already in bed, waiting for her.

She handed him the drink; he took it, smiling; he sipped at it appreciatively, his eyes on her. She put down her own whisky and began to undress. She did it slowly, carefully, teasingly, in the way she knew he liked. The silk of the dress whispered promisingly as it slipped to the floor: his eyes followed her every move, his glance lingering over her bare shoulders, the fullness of her breasts as she cupped them in her hands, the line of her thighs, the smooth flatness of her belly, the shadowed secrets that awaited him, no secrets now.

For some reason, as she moved towards him her mind switched back to the man Jack Tenby had introduced to her that evening: Spate. She doubted whether he would be bedding his colleague tonight, though she guessed he would probably be wanting to. There was something, an undeclared, electric tension between those two. It was something Carrie Fane was aware of: she could read the signs. Her mother had been Norwegian—maybe that was something to do with it. But she could read the signs of sexual attraction, even if unadmitted—and she knew how to please a man.

Like this man.

She slid her naked body onto the bed beside him, drawing back the bedclothes that half covered him. His skin was hot, his eyes excited. She leaned over him, her long hair falling forward, clouding, perfuming his face. Her heavy breasts swung against his chest, touching him lightly and his hands came up to caress them. She kissed him then, lifting herself above him so that she lay along the length of his body. Then, in a little while, she did to him the things he liked, with her hands, with her tongue and with the deep darkness of her thighs.

They did not speak: there was no need for speech. She was a practised lover, and she had been with many men, but this was more than courtesan skills—she enjoyed him, as he enjoyed her. And what they had done together fired her, deepened the relationship, added to the excitement, the danger. In a little while he began to moan and she slowed, deliberately, using her body sinuously, raising his excitement to fever pitch and then holding him off until her own long, slow surge began to climb.

The hardness of his stomach muscles excited her: she could feel the tension rising in him and she began to lose control, feeling her own responses echoing his. A low sound began deep in her throat, presaging the storm; he began to groan himself, his fingers digging into her back, and the pace of their breathing quickened, and then with one quick motion he suddenly swung her sideways, still holding himself inside her, but throwing her on her back. Her arms tightened around him and she began to whisper, meaningless words that they both understood as desire overwhelmed them.

Until suddenly, he stopped moving, his body frozen, hard inside her, but still. She gasped momentarily, confused, and then the new tension in his body was communicated to her. After a few moments, she whispered, 'What is it?'

'*Listen!*'

She lay still, her ears straining, her heart seeming to thunder in her breast. She could hear nothing. She began to relax again. She was about to speak, protest, attempt to recover the slow, sliding rhythm that had been rising to a crescendo of pleasure, when she heard what he had heard.

A light, scrabbling sound. She looked up to the sloping ceiling and the skylight window through which she sometimes, on summer nights, watched the stars. It came again, a scratching, a rat in the attic. Except there was no attic, and no rats.

He withdrew from her. He stared upwards. There was a sudden flash of light, and he yelled, swearing. He ran across the room towards the windows, helplessly, and the noise above had turned to a swift scoring, sliding across the tiles.

Her lover was no longer her lover: he was berserk. His features were torn with fury, he was beside himself with rage. He stood in front of her naked, still aroused, but his fists were clenched as he glared upwards to the ceiling and the skylight and the dawning glow of the early morning sky.

'Bastard!'

She stared at him. She knew raw emotion; she could read his mind. He and Carrie, they had already made a killing.

Now, he was ready to kill again.

'So, Mr Ward, what news you got for me?'

They were standing in the front room of a small terraced house in Fenham. Eric had followed the directions Joe Paulson had given him: drive past the BBC buildings—the *Pink Palace*—turn left into Fenham Hall Drive, and left again. The houses were neat, the doors freshly painted, a street rescued from decay. The Town Moor was not far distant: the city a five minute bus ride away. And the room itself was surprisingly tidy. The three piece suite was old and somewhat battered, but clean; the carpet had seen better days and the window curtains were a little faded but overall the room gave an impression of being reasonably well groomed.

Unlike its owner. Paulson's hair was still lank; his clothes untidy and wrinkled; his general air far from faded elegance. Eric shrugged. 'News? None of it good, I'm afraid.'

Paulson bared his teeth in an unpleasant grimace. He motioned Eric to take a seat, and he perched himself on the arm of the mock leather armchair across from Eric. 'So, tell me.'

'I've done as you asked. I've made a few visits; made a number of phone calls.'

'The editors,' Paulson interrupted eagerly, 'the reporters. What did they have to say? They'll speak in my defence?'

Eric shook his head. 'I'm afraid not. Oh, they all admit to knowing you. Or of you. But not one of them admits to actually having any business connection with you.'

The hunted look in Paulson's face confirmed his anxiety. 'Oldfield at the *Mail*? Stephens at the *Chronicle*? The names I gave you—'

Eric watched him silently for a moment, aware of the anger that was building in Paulson's slitted eyes. 'I tried them all.'

'What about the businessmen, and the politicians I mentioned? Partington at the Carnington Centre? Carlton Dowd? Trevor White?'

Eric had been surprised at some of the names Paulson had given him. But the results had all been the same, when he had contacted them. He shook his head. 'They had nothing to say. They insisted they had no connection with you. The quote was common: *never used his stuff.*' He did not add that they had all also been most uncomplimentary about the dustbin-dredging Joe Paulson. Muck-raker was the least offensive term they had used.

Paulson let out a slow, cold whistle, blowing out his gaunt cheeks. His lip curled with deep-felt malice. 'So that's the way it is. Glad enough to get the stories, the warnings, the early breaks, the information about business rivals that I've been able to supply them with. But when the chips are down, they don't want to know. They run for cover. They deny the very reason for my existence.' He took a deep, ragged breath, his restless eyes glazed. 'All right, if that's the way it's going to be . . .'

'The simplest thing to do is to plead guilty, Mr Paulson,' Eric explained. 'As far as I can gather, the police had been warned and security cameras were set up. They have video material that clearly shows you raiding the dustbins and refuse sacks outside at least two offices in the city. All they want to do is to stop you, and they can do it. So why let it grow into a big issue? You're going to lose anyway. A fine, probably an injunction—'

'Big issue, you say? It is a big issue! It's about freedom of information, Mr Ward. It's about bringing fat cats to justice! It's about showing mealy-mouthed politicians up for what they really are! It's about hoisting up hypocrites to the sanctimonious petards of their own making! I told you—I have a mission, a view of public service—and now these bastards who've been getting fat on what I've been feeding them, they're all either too scared or too contemptuous to get involved! Well, life has never been that easy, believe me. Don't they know what I've got? Not just on the people they've been crucifying—but what I've got on them as well.'

He bounded up from his perch and began to march excitedly about the room, his narrow head thrusting forward, pecking at the air as

95

he spoke. 'They think I'm a little man who'll just curl over, stick his legs in the air and die under their criticisms. But I'm not, Mr Ward: I'm a nightwalker and I got a mission and they're not going to stop me. I'll make them sorry they failed me in my hour of need. And money's no object, I kid you not.' He stopped suddenly, glared at Eric as though he sensed a criticism, and waved his hand around. 'I don't live *here*, you know. This is just a small house that's convenient for me. From here I can make my night raids. Do my night walking. But I've got other places, other properties.' His eyes glittered cunningly. 'Come with me.'

He beckoned, crooking his finger with a sly expression in his eyes. Eric followed as he climbed the stairs: there was a small bathroom on the right, at the top of the stairs—beyond that, two bedrooms. Paulson opened the door to the first room. Under the window was a desk; a personal computer sat there, and a box file. Eric stared in surprise around the walls. They were entirely lined, from floor to ceiling, with shelving that was crammed full with box files. And on the wall behind the door were shelves of loose papers, books, company reports, documents of every shape and size and colour. Littered along the floor were other papers, strewn haphazardly, piled indiscriminately.

'Pandora Number One,' Joe Paulson breathed, smiling with pleasure at Eric's astonishment. 'It's only one of three—and it contains some of the stuff that's low level, not particularly important, but stuff I might need some day. But it all starts here: I sift it, get the good stuff, move it to a safer place. My old man, he never threw things away: he used to say if he only found a screw, I'll keep that, might come in handy some time. I've had the same philosophy. I got my small firecrackers here, but it's nothing to what I've got locked away in my other Pandoras. Some of it is dynamite. Like certain dealings in shares that have been going on this last six months or so; like the immigration racket that's been established, with some very important fingers in the pie; like a certain well-known politician who has a liking for twelve year old girls. And boys. Oh, I've got dynamite all right. Which I may, or not may use, at some time. But I'll certainly use it if they cross me.'

Eric gazed around him. 'You say you have three of these . . .'

'Pandoras. And just like Pandora's own box, when I open them, so many of the evils of the world emerge. Lies, crimes, misdemeanours; falsifications, thuggery, forgery, paedophilia, political dealings of an underhand nature— you name it, Mr Ward, and I've probably got it.' He paused, sighing softly. 'Sometimes, it takes a while to find, and my filing system might not be regarded as . . . shall we say . . . scientific . . . but I have a photographic

97

memory. And good fortune. There's not many nights when I don't pick up a sweet little titbit from the skips, back of the theatres, council buildings, legal offices, accountant firms, estate agents . . . you'd be surprised, Mr Ward. They'll all be surprised, the bastards, making an enemy of me.'

Eric hesitated. He did not doubt that Paulson's eccentricity had led him to discover secrets on his night walks: the comments he made had the ring of truth. But he was duty bound to warn him. 'I'd strongly advise you to get rid of this stuff. You say you have three such . . . storage facilities. When you appear in court, they'll want to curb you, but if they know the amount of material you've collected, they might bear down on you even harder.'

'Not if I bear down on them first,' Paulson suggested maliciously. 'I'll have my day in court, Mr Ward, and then, after that, they can all watch out. Because, you know, although they might deny me now, they'll all fall over themselves to take the information I give them. They're the worst kind of hypocrites— do you think a politician won't eagerly accept the dirt that'll cause his opponent embarrassment? And the purveyors of information . . . I've got more than enough on them to make them squirm, too.'

If you can ever lay your hands on it, Eric thought, as he contemplated the vast array of paper that must be contained in all the files on

98

the bedroom shelves and the litter on the floor.

An hour later, he drove north in the afternoon sunshine, heading for Stagshaw. He glanced at his watch: he should be there in good time. He had checked that morning to make sure Dr Armstrong would be present, along with Eddie Ridout, to begin the discussions with Lon Stanley. The preliminary soundings he had made with the Stagshaw lawyers had been promising. Off the record they had suggested that they were prepared to look for some way of settling the dispute. Like Eric, they knew that Stagshaw would be the ones to suffer if a long running dispute went to court. Even after issuing licences, politicians had a tendency to run for cover when the allegations started flying.

Eric arrived at the Stagshaw site some twenty minutes before the meeting was scheduled to start. He took the opportunity to wander around the site, once he had been admitted at the main gate. He inspected the open pits, noted the warning signs and walked around the perimeter fence, looking across the fields towards Ewart Village. Just beyond the fence there was a small building that had once been a farmhouse. It seemed to be unlived in now, though it was in a reasonably sound condition structurally. He walked back slowly to the main office and spoke to the receptionist. She took him to the first floor, and gave him a cup of coffee. Shortly afterwards, the others came in.

Eddie Ridout was first. He seemed pumped up, ready for a fight, tension in his shoulder muscles, his hard-knuckled hands balling instinctively. Dr Armstrong arrived just behind him: thin, dessicated, with a scrawny neck and intelligent, serious eyes. He had a practice on Tyneside, and held a part-time teaching post in the university department of medicine. He was close to retirement, Eric understood, but his mind was sharp and he had strong views about what had been going on at Stagshaw.

A small, rotund man entered, with a belligerent smile and uneasy eyes, introducing himself as James Denton, the Stagshaw site manager. Behind him came the lawyers, two of them, from Anderson and Gilbert. Eric had spoken to one of them on the phone—Tony Walsh. A paunchy young man with an arrogant, self-satisfied air, he smiled vaguely at Eric and nodded. Then they waited, with their coffee cups in front of them, with little to say to each other, until Lon Stanley finally arrived.

He brought an air of confidence and bonhomie into the room. He was of middle height, dressed casually in a grey sweater and slacks. His hair was worn long, prematurely white, his eyes brown, flecked with green. He was affable, greeting each person in the room, shaking hands firmly, and if he was somewhat put out by Eddie Ridout's cool response he did not show it.

'Gentlemen, please, sit down. You all have coffee? Never touch the stuff myself. Sensitive stomach. Glass of warm water is enough-cleans the insides as well as refreshing the palate.'

Eddie Ridout squirmed in his seat. Eric could guess what he was thinking, in view of the poisonous toxins Stagshaw held in the compound outside the office.

It was Tony Walsh who began, once the preliminaries were over, as Lon Stanley sat back, watchfully. 'Stagshaw is amenable to holding this meeting in the hope that we can reach an agreement satisfactory to all parties,' he began. 'I think we can say that for our part Stagshaw has undertaken all the necessary steps, such as the obtaining of appropriate licences for the storage of a list of toxic substances, and the regular opening of the site to inspectors both local and national. At the same time, we also appreciate the strength of the feelings among local residents in the neighbouring villages, and Ewart in particular, and for that reason we are prepared to discuss suitable . . . ah . . . arrangements for compensation—'

'It's not compensation we want,' Ridout interrupted, 'it's closure.'

Walsh raised elegant eyebrows, flicked a non-existent piece of fluff from his cuff and glanced at Eric. 'That, of course, is certainly not on the agenda, but we are perfectly prepared to be reasonable . . .'

He spent the next ten minutes explaining the Stagshaw position, their licensing arrangements, regular inspection operations, and safety procedures. At the end of it he spread his hands, as though to suggest they were doing all that was humanly possible to prevent problems arising, and since they were running a perfectly legal operation, he failed to see what arguments could arise against them. Lon Stanley remained quiet, but watchful behind lidded eyes.

Eric could almost feel the simmering anger emanating from Eddie Ridout's stocky body. He leaned forward, studying his brief for a moment. 'Perhaps I should begin by making a specific reference to something you said. I won't bother reiterating the claim we wish to make, because that is already in your possession. Rather, I'd like to home in on a couple of issues, which we would, of course, wish to be raising in any enquiry, or court action brought by my clients. First of all, you mention your safety procedures . . .'

He looked up. Lon Stanley's features were impassive, but his eyes were suddenly wary.

'You've outlined these procedures, and you claim that they are effective and have passed the relevant inspections, but you don't seem to have been able to prevent various fires breaking out at Stagshaw. From the notes in front of me I have the details of three explosions since 1997, and in one of these there was a considerable escape of highly toxic chemicals which caught fire and burned out of control, resulting in soot and fumes covering farmland between here and Ewart. I might mention the other occasion when the police were called out and sealed off the area. Then there was—'

'Mr Ward.' Lon Stanley leaned forward, almost casually, but his tone was controlled and determined. 'I'd like to keep this meeting on a friendly basis. You have the facts—we have the facts. Some are in dispute. Others are not. Let's not waste time in going over them. Let's try to reach some reasonable compromises, and get on with our lives.'

Eric held his glance for several seconds. Slowly, he said, 'That's fine, Mr Stanley. I was going to ask Mr Ridout to speak. But, maybe we can take some facts as read. You don't want to discuss the reasons why your vaunted fire safety procedures seemed to be unable to prevent several fires breaking out on the premises. All right . . . maybe a discussion of those procedures can await another day, while we look at . . . possible compromises. But there are some compromises that we cannot accept. Such as those relating to the health and safety of people living in close proximity to the Stagshaw site.'

There was a short silence. Lon Stanley's

eyes glittered. He made no reply. His lawyer leaned forward. 'I'm not sure we should really get into—'

'You'll be aware I've invited Dr Armstrong to attend today,' Eric interrupted. 'I thought it would be useful to let you know what our case will be. Not in the best legal tradition, of course, exposing our hand before trial, but in the interests of remaining *friends*, as Mr Stanley suggests, and seeking reasonable compromises. Maybe I could put a few questions to Dr Armstrong. The kind we would wish to pursue in court.'

Lon Stanley opened his mouth, then closed it again. He nodded, almost imperceptibly, when Tony Walsh looked at him for instructions. The site manager, James Denton, squirmed in his seat. It was clear he did not like the way things were proceeding. In the ensuing silence, Eric turned to the elderly doctor.

'I believe you've made a study of the effects experienced by local villagers, Dr Armstong, as a result of the escape of fumes from Stagshaw.'

He was aware of Tony Walsh leaning forward to object, but Lon Stanley raised his hand and the lawyer subsided. Stanley had the sense to know that it would be useful to understand the Ridout case. And Eric wanted to get some facts out on the table, to push through the settlement he was seeking.

Dr Armstong's fingers were long and slim,

104

the backs of his hands marked by brown liver spots. He observed them gloomily. 'I was guided in the first instance by a study made by Colonel Martin—'

'Colonel Martin may be a resident at Ewart Village,' the site manager, James Denton exclaimed, 'but he is hardly qualified to make comments on the waste materials we store at Stagshaw, and we dispute his findings most strongly.'

Dr Armstrong waited for several seconds before continuing. 'As I was saying, I was guided by Colonel Martin's report, but then proceeded to make my own study, partly at the request of the Ewart Village protest group, represented by Mr Ridout here, and partly in pursuance of other researches I have been carrying out at the university.'

Eric nodded. 'Would you like to give us details of some of your findings?'

Armstrong nodded. 'At the last escape of fumes, twenty villagers were treated for head and stomach aches, sore throats and streaming eyes. Some also reported vomiting, diarrhoea and breathing pains.' He eyed James Denton coolly. 'Colonel Martin referred to these effects: I checked them personally with local doctors and the individuals concerned. Colonel Martin's findings were accurately recorded.'

'Did you form a view regarding these symptoms?' Eric asked.

Armstrong's sad glance slipped around the room, fixing briefly on Lon Stanley. 'One has to remember what is stored at the Stagshaw site. Xylene and toluene and other industrial solvents; methylene chloride—used variously for metal cleaning and insecticides; then there is trichlorethylene, which is often found in antifreeze—'

'All properly and safely stored,' James Denton muttered, unwilling to allow the doctor a free run at the facts, and eager to insist that he ran a safe site at Stagshaw.

'And the long term result of the escape of fumes from such materials?' Eric went on, ignoring Denton.

'Most seriously, perhaps, symptoms of arsenic and selenium poisoning.'

'And what would that lead to?' Eric pressed.

Dr Armstrong lifted a narrow shoulder, shrugging. 'Headaches, tight chest, nausea, dizziness. In severe cases, loss of memory, slowness of speech, yellowing skin.' He paused, reflecting. 'Continued exposure to xylene can also lead to bone marrow damage, problems related to concentration, impaired fertility and anorexia. Toluene exposure adds the danger of impaired speech, vision hearing and muscle control. Trichlorethylene can depress the central nervous system, damage liver and lungs and bring on abnormal heartbeat and coma. There may also be peripheral nervous—'

'Dr Armstrong,' Lon Stanley interrupted, leaning forward casually. 'No one in this room will dispute the effects that escape of these toxic substances may have on the human body and nervous system. It's all well enough documented, I'm sure. But I draw attention to something you said—continued exposure can lead to these symptoms. Is that so?'

'That is correct, Mr Stanley.'

'But we would contend there has been no *continued* exposure. Merely occasional outbreaks.' He glanced briefly in the direction of his perspiring site manager. 'Which have been monitored by the police and the local authority responsible for the granting of licences. Our safety procedures have been passed as acceptable. Our licences have been renewed. So we would argue that since we are complying with everything that is required of us, the fact that these symptoms *can* occur is meaningless, legally. Would you agree?'

'There is some evidence of villagers suffering some of the symptoms I mentioned,' Dr Armstrong replied slowly.

'But no evidence of negligence on our part,' the rotund, perspiring site manager insisted.

'That would be for a court to decide,' Eric suggested.

Stanley stared at him; the friendliness had now disappeared, to be replaced with cold calculation. 'I don't think it would make sense for any of us to take this matter for decision by a court. No one would win; no one would gain.'

'Compensation?' Eric argued.

Stanley shrugged carelessly. 'My company is not one that wishes to avoid its social responsibilities. Let something go to law and all sorts of unfortunate things can happen. We would be prepared to enter into discussions with regard to appropriate levels of compensation being made available to affected parties. But of course such payments, such settlements would have to be confidential and final—'

'And should not be taken as admissions of liability,' Tony Walsh added hurriedly. He would clearly have preferred handling this discussion himself, but it was equally clear that Lon Stanley wanted a quick resolution of the issues, and an avoidance of bad publicity.

Eric glanced at Eddie Ridout. He was unconvinced, and Eric knew that though it made sense to avoid a court hearing, Ridout would take a deal of convincing that a settlement should be reached.

'We would, of course, have to discuss any offers that you would be prepared to make with the villagers group. Mr Ridout is here on their behalf,' Eric said, 'and would wish to make a report to them.'

Lon Stanley spread his hands in a gesture of agreement. 'Of course. But it's in all our interests that these issues are resolved quickly and amicably. Mr Walsh, here, and Mr Denton, they have certain papers that I think they would like to place before you. I myself—'

There was a light tap on the door, and a nervous secretary appeared. 'I'm sorry to interrupt, Mr Stanley, but there's a telephone call.'

'For me?' Stanley frowned. 'I left instructions—'

'Not for you, Mr Stanley,' the secretary replied. Her glance flickered around the room. 'It's for Mr Ridout. And it seems it's urgent.'

Eddie Ridout rose to his feet, uncertainly. Lon Stanley waved a hand. 'That's all right, Mr Ridout. Take the call in my office. We'll just have an outline discussion between the lawyers, and then when you return we can get down to the brass tacks.'

Ridout nodded and left the room. Tony Walsh slid a manila folder across the table to Eric. 'This is an outline agreement of the kind we would wish to use—it covers confidentiality, that sort of thing. There are no figures there, of course, because we would want on our side to discuss levels of compensation. But I've produced a breakdown of the kind of payments that have been made in similar circumstances at other sites.'

'Other than our own, he means,' Lon Stanley interrupted. 'We haven't had problems of this kind at our own sites down south.'

James Denton looked uncomfortable as

109

though he felt his managerial capabilities were being criticised.

Eric inspected the file. It was much as he had anticipated: a legally binding agreement that ensured no villager would be able to speak out of turn if agreed compensation were paid. There was no reference to improved safety procedures; no admission of liability; no agreement on site closure. It would be a difficult agreement to sell to the villagers protest group, but he felt that they would have to be presented with the facts and realities of life: a long court case could cause them years of dispute and heartache—with no guarantee of success at the end.

He continued to read the document and the supporting papers, for a few minutes. Then, just as the door opened to allow Eddie Ridout re-entry to the room, he said, 'Well, of course, the actual levels of compensation are crucial. We'll need to look at exactly how much would be paid, and any compromise or settlement—'

Eddie Ridout interrupted him. His voice was cold, his anger vicious, directed towards Lon Stanley. 'There'll be no compromise, no settlement as far as I'm concerned.'

'Now, Mr Ridout—' Stanley began.

'No compromise,' Eddie Ridout snarled. 'That call, it was from the hospital.' He stood four-square, glaring at Lon Stanley, his solid, stocky body tensed, the strips of greying, reddish hair seeming to stand out from his head with fury. 'It was about my son. He's dead. And it's you—and this bloody site—that killed him.'

There was a short, shocked silence. Lon Stanley seemed riveted to his seat; Denton's pale face was panicked suddenly and Tony Walsh shifted uneasily, glancing at Eric. He seemed to be about to say something, perhaps express sympathy, or denial of legal responsibility. But Ridout was in no mood to accept either.

'You killed my son Sam, with your bloody fumes and incompetence. So don't talk to me of compensation. As far as I'm concerned there'll be no settlement or compromise. I'll see you all in hell first. And as for you, Lon Stanley—watch your back. My son is gone, and you're going to pay. Believe me, you're going to bloody well pay!'

CHAPTER THREE

1

Somewhat perversely, Eric took the long route home. He had not rung Anne, so he was unaware of whether she would be at Sedleigh Hall or not—business matters often called her to London and elsewhere. There were certain documents he needed from his office at Sedleigh, and he also needed some changes of clothing. But he was unwilling to drive there directly—it was as though he feared what he might find.

At first he was barely aware of his surroundings as he headed north into the Simonside Hills: his mind dwelled on the scene at Stagshaw a few days ago when Ridout had stormed out of the meeting after his confrontation with Lon Stanley. Eric had called him since, to express his sympathy as much as anything else, but Ridout had been curt on the phone. Eric had also attended the funeral of Sam Ridout, at the tiny church near the village. Most of the residents had been there but there was no opportunity to spend time with Eddie Ridout, and it was clearly no time to talk business.

As for the Stagshaw people, there had been no communication with them—clearly, they felt the next step must lie with the Ewart villagers in view of Ridout's outburst of fury. Lon Stanley had hinted as much when Eric had left the site: 'There goes any thought of a reasonable solution,' he had remarked drily.

By the time Eric's Celica had breasted the steeper, well-drained slopes of the hills, and crossed the swards of common, covered in velvet bents and sheep's fescue, he had begun to feel more at ease, and able to take some enjoyment in the surroundings. It was up here that he and Anne had taken pleasure in long walks, on the stable rock ledges where harebell, wood sage and golden rod grew. The peregrine falcons were rare up there, since they favoured the grassy hillsides further down on the fells, but there were occasional buzzards, kestrels and sparrowhawks to be seen.

In spring and early summer, near Alwinton they had often taken the hill track, leading their mounts, scrambling up the scree slopes to look back over the open hills and valley sides, to listen to the bubbling call of the curlew, heralding the late-arriving northern spring, or the summering lapwings returning to the high fells from the coast. There were feral goats on these uplands and deer sheltering among the relict oak, birch and ash woodland. He and Anne had spent many leisure hours in the area, but it now all seemed so long ago. His work on the Quayside, and her activity in

113

overlooking the expansion of Morcomb Estates, had somehow left little time of late for the simple pleasures of riding and walking in the hills. But whether that was a symptom or the consequence of the disease itself he could not be sure.

There was no doubt they had grown apart, emotionally. There was no doubt their marriage was crumbling. But whether it was yet capable of being saved was a question he could not answer, and was even unable to face. There was a shadow between them, and its darkness had intensified, but it was as though both of them were unable to prevent that darkness. The words were simply not there.

When he finally caught sight of Sedleigh Hall he felt numb.

He drove up the long curving gravelled drive and rasped to a halt outside the main entrance. Sunlight dappled the meadow edges where the beech trees grew; the stream sparkled as it wound its way across the field, and the Cheviots themselves were shimmering in a lifting haze. He entered the hallway, and was walking towards the stairs when Anne came out of the library.

'Eric! I wasn't expecting you.'

There was no criticism in the tone and yet he felt absurdly guilty. He shrugged. 'I didn't know whether you'd be here.'

She glanced over her shoulder towards the library door. 'I've been involved in a business

114

meeting. I persuaded the board of Martin and Channing it would make a nice change to meet here, rather than in London. They readily agreed.' She observed him carefully. 'I saw your car drive up. You're looking tired.'

He shook his head. 'A bit of midnight oil. Things are pretty busy at the Quayside. And there's the Stagshaw business.'

'I heard that Mr Ridout's son had died.' She looked at him soberly. 'I imagine that will complicate things.'

'More than a little.'

They stood there awkwardly, tongue-tied, like two teenagers not yet versed in the niceties of polite conversation. She was wearing a light blue dress, simple, neat; there was a glint of red in her hair, and her eyes seemed sad as she gazed at him. There was a new beauty about her since those early days when they had ridden the fells together; she was more mature, there was a deeper wisdom in her eyes. As he stared at her, she suddenly said, 'I missed you, Eric.'

There was just one long moment when he could have responded; it grew out of the silence between them as he held her glance, and he took one step towards her, raising his hand. Then the library door opened behind her, he heard a booming laugh, and Jason Sullivan stepped into the hallway, looking back over his shoulder. Eric stopped, Sullivan turned, saw Eric, and the moment was gone.

'Eric! We weren't expecting you.'

The use of the word *we* cut at him like a sword slash. He looked at Anne and saw a brief frustration rise in her eyes, but then it was gone as Sullivan approached. 'The members of the board thought it might be a convenient time to break for a coffee and a smoke,' Sullivan explained easily. 'If that's all right with you, Anne.'

'Of course,' she murmured, still looking at Eric. Sullivan appeared not to notice the tension between them. He stood lounging just behind her left shoulder, smiling at Eric. He was the younger of the two lawyers—more Anne's age. He had a quick smile that he used often, keen grey eyes, and rebellious fair hair that gave him a boyish appearance, flopping over his forehead with careful carelessness. He was still fit: regular squash kept his figure lean and trim; his talents as a lawyer were well recognised in corporate circles: he had taken silk very young. He was suave, confident in manner and graceful in conversation. But Eric had seen the steel in him in the courtroom, and knew that he could be a formidable adversary

'So what's the latest news from the Quayside?' Sullivan asked, managing to inject a certain light contempt into the words. 'Still busy, or are you taking advantage of a slack time today to play the landowner in the hills?'

The tone was bantering, but Eric was aware

116

of the challenging undercurrent. Sullivan knew that there was a problem between Eric and Anne—and he could hardly be unaware that he was largely the cause of it. It lay there unspoken, but recognised by all three.

Eric turned away. 'Still busy,' he responded, heading for the stairs. 'Dealing with real people.'

'Eric!' Anne's tone was sharp, as though she was annoyed, but it might not have been at him. She seemed flustered by Jason Sullivan's presence, as though she felt the need to explain something but could not find the words. 'Will you be staying for dinner?'

He shook his head. 'No, I've got to get back this afternoon. And I wouldn't want to disturb your meeting. I'll just collect a few things . . . but I'd like a word with you before I go.'

The meeting was breaking up in the library: two men came strolling out. Eric recognised them both: Andrew Martin, who was now chairman in place of Leonard Channing, and Norman Wright, an accountant who had been involved in various property speculations over the years, of the kind that left Eric somewhat suspicious. They both greeted him, as though they were old friends—which they had never been. Eric's experience as Anne's representative on the board had never been an easy one under Leonard Channing's chairmanship, and it would have been the same under Andrew Martin, had he stayed. Now it

117

was Jason Sullivan who looked after her interests.

He continued up the stairs, after a brief acknowledgement of their greeting, and went to his room, where he packed a case with some clothing. He found the papers he was looking for in his office, and stuffed them into a briefcase. Then he sat in the chair in front of his desk and stared gloomily out of the window. He felt depressed, haunted by something he could not identify, and in his chest there was a slow burning resentment at the confidence and ease with which Jason Sullivan seemed to have swaggered into his life and home.

He stayed there for an hour or more, listlessly, until at last there was a light tap on the door. It was Anne. She came in hesitantly. 'You got everything you want?'

'Sure.'

'How are things at the flat? No problems?'

'None. I don't seem to spend much time there, in fact—just get my head down at night. Things have been pretty busy.' He wondered whether she detected any of the lies in what he said: the evenings were long in Gosforth, and lonely. Too much time to churn over problems, and growing resentments.

She wandered over to the window, looked out over the meadow and the stream below. 'The board members, they drove up here last night. The meeting will last a couple of days, I reckon. I'm sorry you can't stay over.'

'I'd only be in the way. You're tied up with the business.'

'Maybe that's the problem, Eric.' She turned to face him. 'For both of us.'

'Maybe.' But there was more to it than that; she knew it and so did he. There was the spectre of a dead call girl for him, and for her a time in Singapore, with Jason Sullivan.

'Anyway,' she said, somewhat tight-lipped as though she had read his mind, 'you said you wanted a word with me before you drove back to Newcastle. Anything important?'

He was not fooled by the casual tone. He shrugged. 'I wanted to talk to you about Jason Sullivan.'

'Oh?' She was suddenly on the defensive, as though expecting trouble. 'And what about him?'

Slowly, Eric said, 'It's come to my attention that he was involved with a marine insurance company before he joined the board of Martin and Channing.'

'I wouldn't know about that. I am aware he was involved as a corporate adviser to a number of business clients. That's what made him valuable to Morcomb Estates, when you decided to step out of the job of looking after my interests on the board.'

He was reluctant to respond to the jibe. 'When you asked him to take a seat on the board, did he talk to you about any possible conflict of interest?'

She frowned. 'What do you mean, conflict of interest? Morcomb Estates had no previous dealings in which Jason was involved. I don't understand—'

'I was approached by a journalist recently,' Eric said. 'He asked me various questions about Martin and Channing, and about a ship called the *Princess Eugenie*.'

There was a short silence. Anne frowned. 'The matter of the *Princess Eugenie* is actually on the agenda for the board meeting today.'

'Why?'

She stared at him, frostily. 'I don't think I can discuss that with you, Eric. It's a confidential matter; I can't talk about such matters outside the board room. You stepped down—'

'For God's sake,' Eric snapped, exasperated. 'I'm your husband!'

'Who chose to leave me high and dry as far as my business interests are concerned! And who chooses to live away from me in Newcastle! And who can't admit that his own stubbornness in running a measly practice on the Quayside, dealing with the scum of the Tyne, is affecting our marriage!'

'You know it's not as simple as that!' he responded angrily. 'And as for looking after your interests, that's exactly what I'm trying to do right at this moment. I'm trying to warn you—'

'About Jason? All right—tell me what's

bothering you about Jason!'

'What's bothering me is that you might be getting involved with someone who's under investigation at this moment!'

'And what precisely does that mean?' she demanded, her eyes blazing with fury.

Eric felt he wanted to lash out. She was challenging him, almost as though she did not believe him or his motivation. 'I don't know what it means, *precisely!*' he snapped. 'All I can tell you is what I've heard—'

'From a journalist,' she sneered. 'Oh, come on, Eric!'

He took a deep breath. 'You're not inclined to tell me why the matter of the *Princess Eugenie* is on the agenda of the Martin and Channing board. All right, maybe there's good reason for that, in the interests of company confidentiality. So I'll just try to tell you what I've heard—from a *journalist.* I was asked about Sullivan because it seems that quite apart from the suspicious events surrounding the loss of the *Princess Eugenie,* there were in fact two marine insurance contracts out on her. Martin and Channing were underwriting the insurance of the vessel itself, but there was another contract relating to its cargo. And there is evidence that the cargo was transhipped, before the ship went down.'

'So?'

'So can't you see the problem? There's the likelihood of fraud. There's the possibility that the cargo insurers were involved in that fraud. It seems that Jason Sullivan was a member of the board of the company insuring the cargo. And now he's on the board of the company that insured the vessel itself. When that company is discussing the loss of *Princess Eugenie.*'

'He was put on the board by me!' she flashed. 'Because of his abilities. Because of his skills. Because he was prepared to help a friend. He didn't seek to gain a seat on the board.'

'Oh, don't be so naïve, Anne! There are ways of getting what you want without being too obvious!'

She was silent for a while, glaring at him, her bosom heaving with suppressed anger. He knew that she was reading more into his last words than he had meant; she felt he was criticising Jason Sullivan for the manner in which he had been getting close to her, perhaps using their friendship to gain something more. At last, taking a deep breath, she said, 'Evidence. You suggested there was evidence of underhand dealing. So tell me about it. What evidence?'

He hesitated. He knew he was on shaky foundations. 'I can't tell.'

'Why? Because all you have is unsubstantiated rumours from a gutter journalist?'

'It's not like that,' Eric replied stubbornly.

'Look, it may well be that there is no foundation to what I've heard. It may well be that the enquiry into the sinking of the *Princess Eugenie* will bring up no suspicious circumstances. It may also be that there's no real proof that the cargo was transhipped, and that there's no real evidence of any fraud.'

'Or conflict of interest,' she insisted.

'All right, that too,' Eric admitted. 'But all I'm trying to do is warn you that there are comments, rumours, suspicions, call them what you will, going the rounds. Questions are being asked. And I don't want you being involved in such rumours.'

She shook her head violently. 'No, that's not it, Eric. I think I know what's behind all this— and it has nothing to do with my good name, or with Martin and Channing, or even with the sinking of the *Princess Eugenie.* It's all to do with you and me. And the part that Jason Sullivan is playing in our lives.'

'Anne, I don't want—'

'It's not a question of what you want! It's a question of reality. And the reality is that while I was away in Singapore something happened to you in Newcastle. I don't want to know what it was, but it seems to have soured you, changed your attitudes towards me, and fuelled the resentment you feel because Jason Sullivan was with me in Singapore, that he helped me solve a business problem, that he has a role to play in my life—'

'But what role?' Eric interrupted, regretting the words almost before they had left his lips.

She was silent, breathing hard. 'That's really what this is all about, isn't it? Not that damned ship, not rubbish about marine contracts. It's about you trying to drive a wedge between me and Jason.'

'Do I need to drive a wedge?' Eric asked quietly. 'Are you really that close to each other now?'

The silence between them grew until it was almost unbearable. At last, she said, 'I can't go on with this, Eric. I can't take this resentment, this jealousy, this pettiness. I'm sorry you came back today.'

She wasn't alone in that sentiment, Eric admitted to himself miserably.

* * *

In the late afternoon he drove over the hills towards Ewart Village. His mind was confused: he felt he had been right to voice his concerns to Anne about Jason Sullivan but possibly he could have handled it better. On the other hand, he resented the way she had defended the lawyer, decided so quickly that Eric's motives were suspect, rooted in jealousy.

But then, perhaps they were.

He drove down the hill to Eddie Ridout's farm. It presented a lonely, desolate appearance. Nothing much could have changed physically at the farm since his last visit, and yet with the death of Sam Ridout it was as though an air of loss and desperation had settled there. Ridouts had lived here for generations, but after Eddie there would be no Ridouts.

There was no sign of life, apart from a few chickens scratching in desultory fashion at the side of the house. Eric walked up to the front door and knocked. The noise echoed in the interior as though it was empty, and uninhabited. Eric walked around to the back, looked out to the barn and across the fields, but there was no sign of the man he was seeking. He went back to the car and sat there for a while, as the light began to fade. He was in no hurry; nothing of importance was waiting for him in Gosforth, and he felt dulled, unwilling to move, his mind still churning with the problems facing him and his wife.

After a while, he pulled himself together. Sitting miserably here at Ridout's farm achieved nothing—and it was clear he could be waiting for hours before Eddie Ridout returned. He started the engine, pulled away from the farm entrance and turned back up the hill, heading back south towards Newcastle.

He had just reached the first lift of the fell, with the village of Ewart down below him, when he heard the boom. He looked back, and saw the pall of black, drifting smoke, thick and oily, a hammerhead cloud rising slow and high above Stagshaw.

*　　　*　　　*

It was as though a great storm had rushed through the site, lifting and twisting walls and roofs in its path, throwing debris high in the air, driving a hurricane wind across the enclosure, and producing in its wake a wild display of pyrotechnics, red, and orange, green and blue and yellow. The cloud hit the fire to produce a plume of flame that soared hundreds of feet into the evening sky. The first explosion was followed by a series of smaller explosions, each providing incandescent flares as pockets of flammable gas were hit by flying sparks. The sheds were blown sky-high, disintegrating under the sudden thunder of the explosion; the open pits were suddenly sheeted with flame and a deadly cocktail of fumes and smoke curled upwards, higher and higher, a black pall of smoke lit from within by flashes of light, fire being driven and ignited by a two hundred mile an hour gale.

The conflagration seemed to produce its own whirlwind, and as two more explosions followed the scene became an inferno, a whirling mass of noxious gas that produced a purple rain drifting towards the village and farms beyond Stagshaw.

Then, almost miraculously, it seemed to be

126

over, only a matter of minutes after it had begun. The wind dropped, the fire flickered and faded, the breeze lifted and the black and purple cloud began to thin, and drift, fading away seawards, to the distant coast. A vast silence enveloped the area; the black, twisted, charred remains of what had been Stagshaw lay still and quiet as the moon rose, low above the fell, gleaming fitfully through the dissipating cloud, flickering over the desolation of a battlefield.

2

'Do you really find all men boring?' Charlie Spate asked.

Elaine Start shook her head. 'Not all men. Some are dead.'

That was the problem with her, Charlie thought to himself. Too bloody smart by half. But she bothered him nevertheless; he couldn't make her out sometimes, and though she had rejected his advances the other evening, and though he knew it would be a mistake to have another crack at her, he was still plagued with thoughts about her legs, her body and her mouth . . . He grunted, annoyed with himself and he walked past her desk towards the corridor. He had the feeling she was staring at his back, half-smiling.

The Chief Constable was waiting for him in his office. He kept Charlie waiting for a few moments before he invited him to take a seat. He was a big man, with a military air, reputed to have failed his law degree before he'd joined the Met and made his way up through the ranks. He was unusual for top brass, in that he liked to keep his finger on the pulse of things, a habit Charlie found irritating since it meant he was constantly being asked to report on what he was up to. On the other hand, he supposed he owed the Chief Constable something: it had been by way of returning a favour that the Chief had agreed to take Charlie on when he was advised to leave the Met, and permitting him retention of his rank.

'So, DCI, how's it going—your new assignment, I mean?'

'Not a great deal to report, sir,' Charlie replied. 'Blanchard's not talking, of course, but that was to be expected.'

'Because of the injuries he sustained to his face?' the Chief Constable asked sarcastically.

'Because he's a hard nut, sir,' Charlie said, refusing to rise to the bait. 'We've got him nailed with the evidence, so he'll take the porridge and keep his mouth shut. Probably well advised to do so, as well: there's some hard cases breathing down his neck out there. The kind that can sort a man out, inside or outside the slammer.'

'But you have no leads as to who is behind the drug shipments?'

Charlie Spate eyed the man in front of him:

he had a Welsh background it seemed, and when he got angry, or Wales lost at rugby, he had a tendency to let some of his vowel sounds slip. Charlie knew that it could happen now. 'Oh, I'm pretty sure that we all know who's behind the recent surge, sir.'

The Chief Constable scowled, and sighed. 'It's a fixation you got, Spate.'

'No, sir, it's talk along the river. Mad Jack Tenby has his legitimate enterprises, that we know. And they're not cover for other things. But the word is that however much he protests his innocence, and how he's reformed—now that he's moving in better circles—he's still a villain at heart and wanting to get his hands dirty like the old days.'

'He was never into drugs,' the Chief Constable demurred. 'A hard man, yes, but not drugs.'

'Only because he was old-fashioned, ran the clubs and prostitution business—and saw the light too soon to get involved when the drugs scene opened up. But now, with the break-up of the syndicate last year, I think he's seen his opportunity. I'm damned certain he was behind that haul we got the other night.'

The Chief Constable sighed wearily, stroked his chin with an irritated hand. 'Well, all I'm saying to you, Spate, is go carefully. Tenby has a lot of connections now and a lot to lose. Before you do anything foolish, check with me.'

Because we wouldn't want any of your own political and county connections to start jumping up and down, Charlie thought to himself.

'And what about that other thing,' the Chief Constable went on after a short, uncomfortable silence. 'That young man . . .'

'Terry Bell,' Charlie offered. 'The Batboy. Not a sign of him. But then, he's managed to evade Tyneside's best over the years.'

The Chief Constable scowled at the thought. 'He'll turn up, no doubt, and we'll get him. Do you think he'll be able to help the investigation?'

Charlie shrugged. 'I'd like to talk to him. The scuttlebutt is that he's no hero, and he might be prepared to grass now that he'll be facing a stretch himself. If we can get hands on him, maybe he'll have something to tell us. I got the feeling that Blanchard and his crew didn't know the kid was stashed away up there in the loft. They've made no mention of him. I think the little bugger was up there for his own ends, and no good they'd be either. But he could tell us something useful. If we can get hold of him by the scruff.'

'Yes, well, keep at it,' the Chief Constable said doubtfully. He drummed thick fingers on the desk in front of him. 'How many you got in your team at the moment?'

'Five, sir.'

'Hmm.' The Chief Constable thought for a

moment. 'We're going to have to strengthen the team.'

'I'm grateful, sir, but is that necessary? The lines of enquiry we're following—'

'No,' the Chief Constable interrupted. 'I want it strengthened, not just to follow up the drugs shipments. I'm putting another job on your plate.'

Charlie Spate grimaced, but said nothing.

'You'll be aware there was an explosion up at Stagshaw a couple of days ago,' the Chief Constable explained. 'We sent a team up there to do a preliminary investigation. It was damned lucky no one was killed, but it seems the explosion occurred shortly after the staff had left, and before the watchman arrived. Some security arrangements,' he grunted contemptuously, 'but there you are. Bloody amateurs. Anyway, the early reports are that it looks as though it might have been accidental but there's a strong suspicion it could have been deliberate.'

'Arson?' Charlie Spate widened his eyes innocently. 'Now why would they be thinking that, sir?'

'It isn't often that two hundred tons of carcinogenic toxic waste goes up in the air,' the Chief Constable suggested.

'But accidents can happen.'

'This was a toxic waste dump. It had given rise to a certain . . . controversy. There's been a couple of smaller explosions, or fires, over the years—nothing really serious like this one. As it happens, even this one was not as serious as it could have been—the fire never really expanded, and the fumes tended to drift reasonably harmlessly out to the coast.'

'Are toxic chemicals ever reasonably harmless, sir?'

The Chief Constable's eyes were blue ice as he glared at Spate. 'The fact is, we've had information to the effect that the explosion might have been deliberate. We haven't found the seat of the fire yet, but in a nearby village there's a protest group, and you know what can happen when such groups get together. And the owner has given us information to the effect that one man in particular might be said to have a strong enough grudge to take action of this kind.'

'The owner would be . . .?'

'A man called Stanley. Details of his statement are in this file.' The Chief Constable pushed the folder across the desk to Charlie. 'Better check it out.'

'Have we interviewed the person described as having a grudge against . . . Mr Stanley?'

'No. That's the other thing. He's disappeared. So get on to it. If we can wrap this thing up quickly, it would be as well.'

Because if we don't, some influential people might get irritated, Charlie thought, as he inspected the contents of the folder. Like Mr Stanley, the London-based owner and likely subscriber to charitable causes. Like the politicians who issued the licences for the waste site. And the civil servants and chief executives who hadn't kept a tight enough control on their inspection arrangements. And even . . . 'Do we know what actually went up in the explosion, sir?' Charlie asked.

'I told you. Chemicals. Quite a cocktail. They're listed in there.'

'Them going up together,' Charlie mused, 'it must have been a sight that would have delighted the heart of a commander on the Somme.'

'Never mind the pyrotechnics. Find out if it was deliberate. And if it was, bring the culprit to book. To start with, work with just one officer.'

Just the kind of job for Elaine Start, Charlie thought maliciously. Get her bloody hands a bit dirty, shuffling through charred rubbish. Break a few nails, curb a smart tongue. He'd have pleasure telling her about her new assignment.

*   *   *

She did not take to it at all kindly.

She seemed happy enough to take the drive out to Stagshaw, in the first instance. Nor was she particularly bothered when they walked around the site, assessing the extent of the damage. The sheds were blown apart; the open pits filled with rubbish; a fine dust

133

obscured everything, and a team was busy sifting through the ash, inspecting drums that had not gone up in the conflagration. It was when the wind picked up slightly, raising the dust so that it drifted about the site, getting in hair and eyes and mouths that she began to get unhappy. She was even unhappier when he told her she could stay there the rest of the day, help the team and keep an eye on things while he followed up the leads in the folder he had been given. One of them would take him back to Newcastle.

'But how will I get back to town, gov?' she complained.

He gestured towards the men in yellow overalls and masks. 'Get a lift from one of them boring buggers,' he suggested.

He left her and walked the perimeter. The fence was down, blown away in the blast. It was a scene of complete devastation. He stood there contemplatively, staring at the small farmhouse, burned out just beyond what had been the perimeter fence. He walked across to the truck in which sat a small, dark-moustached man, writing in a notebook. 'You forensic?'

'That's right. And you are?'

'DCI Spate. Any new thoughts on what happened up here?'

The little man grimaced. 'It was a big bang, I'll tell you that. So big, I think it actually blew out some of its own conflagration. If that's unscientific enough an explanation for you.'

Oh, yes, smart-arse. 'What about that old farmhouse over there?'

'Uninhabited. Looks like it caught only part of the blast, and burned out. We've been concentrating on the site first; we'll get around to the farmhouse later today, I expect.'

'And was it arson?'

'Too soon to say. They heard the drums of chemicals exploding a mile and a half away. But the whole thing could have started with something as simple as a drop of water falling into a vat of acid. And if the safety procedures weren't all they should have been, that's exactly what might have happened. I mean, those open pits . . . Depends on what's stored in them, of course. And there are a few drums that didn't go up, so we've got to take a look at those. All I will say at the moment, you couldn't have found a more toxic assortment of chemicals to blow up if you tried. But it could have been accidental.'

'Seat of the fire?'

'As yet, not known. But we'll tell you, Mr Spate, we'll tell you.'

'Hmmm.' Charlie was suddenly aware that Elaine Start was at his elbow.

She glanced around at the site, before facing him. 'I just thought you'd like to know I've managed to cadge a lift back, sir. And he doesn't seem very boring.'

'That's nice for you. But I wasn't waiting

135

around to find out if you were walking back or not.'

She looked away from him scanning the devastation of the site, ignoring the comment. 'Funny how things happen in an explosion, isn't it?'

'Things get flattened.'

'But not all things. Take that farmhouse, now. Burned, yes, but some of the walls are still standing. You'd have thought they'd get flattened too.'

It was something that had already crossed his own mind. But forensic could have a look at that. It was time he got back to Newcastle.

*   *   *

Charlie Spate parked his car at the water's edge, near the Millennium Bridge, and spent a few minutes watching the workmen welding the stanchions along the walkway, sparks flying and falling to the dark waters below. There was pride, as well as a lot of money had gone into that bridge, he thought to himself—and hoped it would work better when finished than the new footbridge across the Thames. He sighed. There were times when he was happy to be away from the Met.

He walked away from the riverside towards the old Exchange building that housed Eric Ward's office. The lawyer's secretary didn't seem too pleased when she recognised him, but he didn't fancy her anyway. 'Mr Ward available?'

'I'll check, Mr Spate,' she replied with just an edge of frost in her tone.

He waited while she checked. When she advised him that her employer would be able to see him it was with an air that suggested he was a very lucky man. He walked into Ward's office and sat down without invitation.

'An unexpected visit, Mr Spate,' Ward said, implying in his tone it was no pleasure.

Charlie grinned. 'Just thought I'd call in to see how you were getting on in your vibrant practice.'

'It's busy enough.'

'With people like Joe Paulson? How is that little ratbag, anyway? Still pleading his value to society and social justice?'

Eric Ward's eyes were wary. 'Is it Paulson you've come to see me about? The hearing isn't scheduled—'

'Nah, I'm not interested in that little weasel,' Charlie interrupted. 'Though I might be, if he was able and prepared to give me information on the drugs operation on Tyneside. You think he could do that?'

'I'm sure I wouldn't know.'

'Well, he's reckoning he's got a lot on all the big boys along the Tyne. He given you no chat about Mad Jack Tenby?'

Eric Ward regarded him quietly for a few moments. 'If this is a fishing expedition, Mr

137

Spate, I'm afraid the fish aren't biting.'

'Ah, client's privilege,' Charlie said wisely. 'I just thought you might be prepared to help me out here and there, since we're mates and all that.'

'I wouldn't quite describe our relationship in those terms,' Ward replied drily. But Charlie saw the shadow in his eyes, and knew it was as well to remind the lawyer from time to time that there was a debt between them. And one of these days, maybe Charlie Spate would call it in.

'No, well, maybe you're right. Fact is,' Charlie went on with a resigned air, 'it seems our paths are crossing again, not so much about Joe Paulson, but about a certain explosion that occurred a few days ago.'

There was a short silence. After a while, Eric Ward said, 'You're referring to Stagshaw.'

'I am indeed. You do get around, don't you? It seems that when our lads got to the scene of the . . . incident, you were already there. Helping out, so to speak.'

'That's right.'

'Bit away from the Quayside, wasn't it?'

Ward hesitated. 'I'd been up to my home at Sedleigh Hall. I was on the way back to Newcastle, when I heard the explosion, saw the plume of smoke. So I went down, to see if there was any way I could help.'

'Mmmm. Sedleigh to Ewart Village. Bit of a roundabout way, returning to Newcastle. What

138

was it—taking in the scenery?'

'I've been known to do it,' Ward replied carefully.

'But I don't think that was really the way of it, Mr Ward.' Charlie sighed. 'I get the impression that your practice tends to deal with losers. And I hear that you had been retained by the protest movement up at Ewart Village. They been trying to get Stagshaw closed down. You reckon that brief would have been one of your winners?'

'I would have hoped so.'

'But now that's all . . . up in the air, hey?' Charlie bared his teeth, amused by his own witticism. 'I mean, if there was direct action, so to speak, you'd be losing out on your fees, wouldn't you? The Stagshaw site would close down anyway—at least for a while. And maybe it would never open again.'

'Just what are you getting at?' Ward asked quietly.

'Aw, I just wondered whether your people up at Ewart, feeling they didn't want to go through the long, involved process of a hearing, decided it would be simpler to torch Stagshaw and get their own way without any more argument.'

'Have you evidence that arson was involved?' Ward asked sharply. 'There've been at least three explosions at Stagshaw over the last few years. It's more than likely that this was another accident.'

Charlie shrugged. 'That could be, of course. But at this stage, we don't know. And me, I've only just taken over the investigation and haven't got my feet under the table yet. Haven't spoken to everyone involved. Like your client . . . what's his name, Ridout?'

Ward was silent for a little while. Then he shrugged. 'Eddie Ridout isn't exactly my client. I mean, I've been retained by the Ewart protest group. It just so happens that Ridout is their spokesman.'

'Not saying too much at the moment, is he?'

'What do you mean?'

'I mean he's done a bunk. Disappeared. Vanished into the thin.' Charlie Spate watched Eric Ward carefully. 'Now why do you think he would do that?'

'I don't know that he has . . . disappeared.'

'Well, he has. Take my word for it. But my guess is you maybe went to see him the day of the explosion. That's why you were in the area.'

Ward remained silent, thinking.

'*Did* you go to his farmhouse that afternoon?' Charlie persisted.

Reluctantly, Eric Ward nodded. 'I . . . wanted to see him on a personal matter.'

'To express your condolences, maybe?' Charlie nodded. 'I heard that he'd just buried his son. But when you called, did you see him at the farmhouse?'

After a slight hesitation, Eric Ward shook his head. 'No. I tried at the house, looked

140

around, but he wasn't at home.'

'Maybe he was down at Stagshaw.'

'He could have been anywhere,' Ward argued.

'Yeah, I know that, but he was involved with the Stagshaw dispute, and he'd just buried his son—who he reckoned had been killed by exposure to toxic fumes from the waste site— and he was, by all accounts, mad as hell about it. The afternoon Stagshaw goes up he's not at home, and since then he's simply not to be found. Hey, Mr Ward, you know what it looks like? Doesn't it add up to something?'

'Not a lot. You don't even know if the explosion was caused deliberately, yet.'

Charlie smiled. 'That's right, that's right. But if we do come up with the evidence, well, try to persuade Eddie Ridout to get in touch with us. Running away don't help, if you're under suspicion. So when you see him, tell him to get in touch.'

'*If* I see Mr Ridout,' Eric Ward said calmly, 'I certainly will.'

Charlie Spate nodded, and stood up. 'Well, since there's no sign of any coffee, and if you don't have anything more to tell me, I suppose I'd better get back.'

He sauntered off, whistling as he made his way down the stairs.

*　　　*　　　*

141

After he had gone, Eric rose and walked across to the window, to stare out across the river to the Gateshead bank. Dark clouds were scudding in from the sea: there could be a storm tonight. He realised his hands were shaking slightly and he guessed that in a little while the pain behind his eyes would start again, unless he took some medication soon. He grunted in frustration. Meeting DCI Spate was always a somewhat unsettling experience. It was linked to the events of six months ago. He had been forced to tell Spate of his part in the death of the call girl, but the information given had never become common knowledge. Spate had never revealed it, for reasons of his own. But Eric guessed that it was merely kept as some kind of card that Spate held—and it worried him that one day Spate might want to play the card, and Eric Ward would be the loser.

As for Eddie Ridout . . . Eric went back to his desk and picked up the phone. He dialled Ridout's farmhouse. There was no reply. It worried him. The thoughts that were occurring to Spate had already occurred to him: Ridout had a strong motive for setting fire to Stagshaw, and in his disturbed state of mind he was certainly capable of doing it.

After a while Eric used the contact number Joe Paulson had given him. The phone rang, unanswered. He smiled grimly. Suddenly, his clients seemed to be disappearing. The prickling at the back of his eyes began to get worse.

There had been a moment, when Charlie Spate was in his room, just a moment when Eric had been tempted to ask the policeman about the *Princess Eugenie.* He had held back— it was too dangerous, exposing his feelings to Spate in that way. If he was to find out anything about the possible involvement of Jason Sullivan with fraudulent practices, talking to Charlie Spate was not the way to do it.

It was all a juggling act: Stagshaw and Eddie Ridout; Anne and her relationship with Jason Sullivan; Sullivan and the loss of a cargo; Joe Paulson, and the men who had denied him. Eric was finding it difficult to concentrate. First, he'd better take some pilocarpine. Then, perhaps, arrange to meet Jackie Parton.

3

The principal route from the Quayside and the mediaeval bridge to the higher parts of the town had always been The Side, making its ascent under the lowering walls of the twelfth century castle built by Henry II and designed by Maurice the Engineer. Eric took it in the early evening, walking from his office past St Nicholas's Cathedral towards the area still designated by the old market names—Cloth Market, Groat Market, Bigg Market. The curving slope of Grey Street took him to the

143

modern part of the town much redeveloped since the days of Richard Grainger and John Dobson, but still alive and bustling and humming with life.

Too much life on Saturday nights, he mused, and sometimes death when the youth gangs spilled out of the pubs to celebrate a Newcastle United win—or defeat—by singing, dancing and fighting. On those nights the Northumberland Fusilier was a pub to avoid, but this was not Saturday and while the lounge bar was fairly busy with regulars, they were mostly professional people, taking a drink before they set off homewards.

Jackie Parton was at the bar. He saw Eric when he came in, nodded, and gestured towards a table in the corner. Eric sat down and a few minutes later Jackie Parton joined him, carrying a pint of Newcastle Brown for himself and a brandy and soda for Eric. They had known each other a long time.

It had been years since Jackie Parton had ridden winners at Newcastle Racecourse but he still had the lean, whippet-like frame he had worked at as a young man. He had grown up at Scotswood where a boy had to be tough to survive and his success on the track as a young apprentice had made him well-known; later, his devil-may-care riding had turned him into a local legend. So when his racing days were over—brought about, it was whispered, by suspicions of bribery, races being thrown, a confrontation with local gambling bosses—he had found a way to live off his wits. His local knowledge was unrivalled: his sporting background gave him entry to the pubs and clubs at Benwell and Byker, Felling and Shields, and his stamping ground was the Tyneside shadowland. He had contacts at all levels along the river; he played no role in the violence and mayhem, the gang warfare and muscle that shifted constantly around the docks and housing estates, but he was known and trusted for not taking sides. Over the years Eric had found him useful—a man who could get reliable information and who could keep his mouth shut. He had used Parton in his police days, and later, when he had qualified as a solicitor Eric had found that the ex-jockey's local knowledge and contacts were extremely valuable.

They had become friends during that period, but the friendship had cooled somewhat recently. Jackie Parton had always admired and respected Eric Ward, for the way he had operated as a policeman, the manner in which he had overcome his physical problems, and for the fact that as a lawyer he was straight. But now he saw him as flawed; his confidence in Eric had been shaken by recent events, he was aware of the crumbling walls of Eric's marriage and the old closeness had gone.

Eric guessed it might never come back.

'It's been a while, Mr Ward. You been keeping busy?'

'Pretty much so.' Eric accepted the drink with a nod of thanks. 'But some of my clients are giving me problems.'

'Ain't that always the case?' Jackie Parton's glance slipped away, checking out who was coming in, and who was leaving. He was always like that, wary, noting his surroundings. 'And I suppose that's why you rang me?'

'That's right. I've no doubt you'll have heard about the explosion up at Stagshaw.'

'The chemical waste site. Should have closed it down years ago, is my view.' Jackie sniffed contemptuously, and took a long pull of his beer. 'But too many people with fingers in the pie, I reckon. Councillors, so-called businessmen, but that was always the way of the world. Here on Tyneside, anyway. So what's your interest in what happened up there?'

Eric explained briefly about the protest group at Ewart Village, their representative Eddie Ridout, the confrontation at Stagshaw, and Ridout's disappearance at the time of the explosion.

'You say his son died in hospital,' Parton said slowly.

'That's right. Stagshaw personnel will argue that his illness and death have nothing to do with the fact that he worked the farm near the site, and maybe it would be difficult to prove a direct connection. But that isn't really the point. Eddie Ridout believes there's a direct link, and he uttered various threats towards the owner of Stagshaw.'

'Then the site blows up, and Ridout disappears.' Jackie Parton scratched his battered nose, kicked by a horse when he had fallen at the third fence, years ago. 'I can see how the minds of the polis will be working. He's not been in touch with you?'

Eric shook his head. 'I haven't heard from him, or seen him since the funeral. He was in a bad way that day: constrained, haggard, withdrawn. He was taking Sam's death very badly.'

'And you want me to try to find him.'

Eric saw the doubt in the ex-jockey's eyes. 'I know it's not exactly your line. Ridout is not a Tynesider, so your contacts might not be able to help. But I thought it was worth a try.'

Jackie Parton shrugged. 'Just give me some time. I know a few landlords out in the county. It's surprising what publicans hear. And there's a few farmers I can talk to—they used to follow the point to points. I did a bit of that as well, you know, in the old days. Maybe they'll come up with something. And anyway, there's a fair bit of talk about the Stagshaw explosion. Information drifts in. I'll see what I can find out.' He was silent for a little while, sipping his drink. 'I hear you got another client who's rather better known along the river.'

'Who would that be?'

'Joe Paulson.'

'You know him?'

Jackie Parton grinned wickedly. 'The nightwalker? Who doesn't? He's like a wharf rat, slipping along in the dark, turning over rubbish dumps, sniffing into plastic bags, oh, believe me, I've come across him. But he's a bit weird, you know? Story is he's got a whole load of stuff stashed away, with dirt on almost everyone on Tyneside—politicians, coppers, charity leaders, churchmen—and all picked up by regular work on the night shift. He's even got stuff on some of the gang bosses, I hear, but I guess he'd never have the nerve to use it. It could lead to his head being bashed in. Can you imagine what would happen if he tried it on with the likes of Mad Jack Tenby? On the other hand, it's a bit of insurance, I suppose, against trouble.'

'Paulson seems to have gone to ground as well, just recently,' Eric remarked. 'He's due to attend a hearing next week, and there might be fireworks there, if he chooses to tell the court what he knows, as part of his defence. But talking of insurance . . . '

Jackie Parton caught the hesitation in Eric's tone and cocked an eyebrow. He waited.

'Have you heard any rumours about a ship called the *Princess Eugenie*?'

'Out of the Tyne?'

Eric shook his head. 'No, out of Wearside, I

148

believe. She sank in the Mediterranean, and there have been certain questions asked about the loss. The ship was covered by Martin and Channing.'

'I see. That's your interest in it. But I thought you weren't with the company any more.'

'That's not quite it,' Eric said cautiously. 'There was another insurance contract taken out, on the cargo. I just wondered whether you'd picked up any rumours along the river, about what happened to that cargo. I'm told that it's whispered the cargo was transhipped before the *Princess Eugenie* went down.'

Jackie Parton considered the matter. 'There's some people I could talk to on the river. I'll see what I can find out. It's a matter of an insurance scam then, is it? Are you acting for the insurers? I need to know, in case I talk to the wrong people.'

Cautiously, Eric replied, 'It's not quite as simple as that. I have no direct interest in the matter. No client actually involved.'

There was something about the emphasis inadvertently placed on the word client, that drew Parton's attention. His glance was sharp. He waited, saying nothing. The silence grew around them.

At last, Eric said, 'I want to know whether there really was a transhipment of that cargo. And I want to know whether Jason Sullivan was involved in any way.'

149

Jackie Parton leaned back in his chair, staring at Eric. They had never talked about what was wrong in Eric's marriage; Jackie Parton knew Anne, and liked her—he felt she never patronised him, she was a lady, and she could occasionally demonstrate a low sense of humour, which appealed to him. And he was concerned about the tensions that had clearly arisen between Eric and Anne. He knew they were partly rooted in Eric's own infidelity some months back. But the sensitive hairs on the back of his neck had risen now. 'Jason Sullivan. The QC.'

'That's right,' Eric replied in a level tone. 'He took over from me when I resigned from the board of Martin and Channing. He's there now as Anne's . . . as the representative of Morcomb Estates.'

Jackie Parton knew there was more to it than he was hearing. He tapped his gnarled fingers on the side of his beer glass. 'So what's the problem?'

Eric shrugged uneasily. They were getting onto difficult terrain. He was beginning to regret raising the matter with the ex-jockey, but it was too late to back down now. 'I've been told that Sullivan was on the board of the company that insured the cargo of the *Princess Eugenie*. He's now on the board of Martin and Channing. If there really was some sort of fiddle going on with the cargo, there's just the possibility there might be a conflict of interest

150

of some kind . . .' His voice trailed away.

After a little while Jackie Parton asked, 'Have you told Mrs Ward about this?'

'I tried to.' Eric gritted his teeth. 'She . . . she didn't take it too well.'

Jackie Parton frowned. He raised a narrow shoulder, dismissively. 'I suppose she made the board appointment, and doesn't want to feel she made a mistake.' But he was suspicious, Eric knew: the ex-jockey was sharp enough to pick up signals that told him this had something to do with the relationship between man and wife. But that was none of his business.

Jackie Parton nodded. 'I got some contacts at the docks. And there's a few characters I know in the shipping offices. I might pick up something, as far as the cargo transhipment goes. But if it's high level stuff I won't be able to get near it.' He paused, thinking. 'But I'll tell you someone who might be able to help, though.'

'Who?'

'Your own client. Joe Paulson. As we know, he picks up all sort of stuff. For instance, the whisper is that he's been sniffing around on some sort of sharedealing scam recently. You know, the recent sharp rise in the Sandhurst Securities, and the launch of that Holystone Mining company? The scuttlebutt is that someone's been making a packet out of those, and other deals, and that Paulson has been hinting that he's got enough to finger someone. So, if he's able to pick up documents on that kind of thing, you'd stand a better chance getting him onto this *Princess Eugenie* problem. He knows his way around that kind of thing. It's really a bit too rarefied for the likes of me.'

Eric knew he was right. But he baulked at the idea. Apart from the fact that Paulson was a client of his, he knew the man and would be more than reluctant to enlist his services. Even if there was a greater likelihood of success. 'No,' he said, 'I don't think I can do that. And if you can't help . . .'

'I didn't say that, Mr Ward. Give me some time. Let me ask around. I can't promise nothing, but maybe I'll pick up something here or there. Another drink?'

'I'll get them,' Eric replied. He rose, went up to the bar and ordered two more drinks. He felt uneasy, unsettled. He had made a mistake asking Jackie Parton to look into the *Princess Eugenie* matter: it would be better if he himself stayed away from the problem that the journalist Karl Preece had raised with him. But it was too late now—it was best to let Jackie find out what he could. Maybe it would come to nothing anyway.

He walked back to the table and put down the glasses, slid into his seat. No more mention was made of the business. They chatted about inconsequential things. Eric was in no hurry to

152

go back to the flat: he had decided he would probably have a meal in town before he went back anyway. So he listened as Jackie talked about the days in Old Benwell and the racing circuit, the fixes that had been put on, the way things had changed. 'In the old days it was muscle and thuggery, betting, gambling, prostitution but it all changed when the drugs started flooding in. It all got nastier, and the killings . . . well, there was killings in the old days, but now it's knives, and people who are so high they'll stick you for no reason. And even the whores are different. You know, in the old days it was a way out of Scotswood for a girl and there was a bit of choice about it. Now, hell, they're shipping the whores in from Eastern Europe and believe me, Mr Ward, they're a sad bunch. Good looking enough, but there's something about them . . . They're dead inside . . . they got no options, no hope . . .'

As Jackie talked about the old days, and about the changes, it was almost as though he and Eric were going back to better times when they were more relaxed with each other, to the days when he had first met the ex-jockey as a copper on the beat, and the days when he had first used his services to obtain information for his clients. The tensions of the last few months were slipping away, and he began to think that maybe the old relationship might yet be re-established.

The ease was suddenly interrupted.

153

'Well, Mr Ward, it seems we just can't stop bumping into each other! People will be starting to talk.'

It was DCI Charlie Spate. He stood in front of them, with a pint of beer in his hand. Eric gained the impression it wasn't the first drink Spate had had this evening. His face was slightly flushed, and there was a slight slurring in his speech.

'I didn't know this was one of your haunts. You here on business, Mr Spate?' Eric asked.

'Haunt? The Northumberland Fusilier? It's as good as any other in town, and better than most. But if you're asking whether I'm a regular here, no that's not so. It's one I can call in, from time to time. Like tonight. The George, the Pot and Pig, the Fusilier here, and then who knows? As for business, hell no. I'm just relaxing. We all have to do it, from time to time.' He eyed Jackie Parton, seated quietly at the table. 'You haven't introduced me.'

'DCI Spate . . . Jackie Parton,' Eric said coolly.

'Parton?' Charlie Spate was silent for a few moments, clicking through the information in his head. 'I heard of you. Bit of a reputation on the track.'

'Years ago, Mr Spate. And I've heard of you.'

'Is that so?' Charlie Spate smiled maliciously. 'I bet none of it's been good.' He glanced at Eric. 'Yes, I remember the talk now.

You used to use Jackie here when you was one of us. And you still do. Legman, ain't that right? Prevents you getting your own lillywhites dirty.' He shrugged, waved his glass. 'Well, I'm still sufficiently sober to be aware that you won't be extending an invitation to me to join you. Besides, you'll probably want to carry on huddling together plotting some skullduggery or other. So I'll leave you to it.'

He nodded in mock affability and walked away from them, back towards the bar. They watched him lean there, begin to talk to the barman. The barman listened, stolidly wiping a beer glass with a discoloured rag. 'You think he's on a bender?' Jackie Parton asked.

'Possibly.'

'They say he's got a wild side,' Parton suggested. 'Rumour is he got the push from the Met. Got too close to some of the villains down there. It's easily enough done, I suppose; it's a trap to avoid. And there's talk about women, too.'

He fell silent. Spate's arrival had interrupted a mood. They neither seemed to want to talk now, and the previous uneasiness had returned. They sat quietly, watching people in the lounge bar. Eric finished his drink, toyed with it for a little while and then decided he would have one more for the road. Jackie Parton hesitated, then agreed to have a short one himself.

Eric walked up to the bar and ordered the

drinks. As he stood there, some feet away from Charlie Spate, who ignored him, he saw a woman enter the room at the far door, look around, and then make her way in his direction. Her face was familiar. When she walked past him, up to Charlie Spate, Eric realised who it was. Detective Constable Elaine Start. She seemed not to notice him as she went up to Spate. Eric overheard their conversation.

'I've been trying to contact you, sir, on your mobile,' she said tightly.

He grinned. 'Switched off. Saving electricity. Everyone's entitled to a little privacy once in a while. And even a pub crawl.' He caught Eric's glance. 'Especially a pub like this where flawed characters like coppers, and lawyers and villains can all meet socially.'

'I need to talk to you, sir,' she said urgently, touching his sleeve.

Eric caught the irritation in her tone. He took the drinks back to the table. Jackie Parton was watching the two detectives, and asked Eric who the woman was. Eric told him. A moment later, as he listened intently, Charlie Spate straightened, staring at his assistant. Then he quickly drained his glass, stood there for a moment, then nodded, and they made their way towards the door. Then, to Eric's surprise Spate stopped, said something to Elaine Start and came back to stand in front of Eric.

He grinned maliciously. 'So you want the

bad news, or the bad news, or the bad news?'

'What are you talking about?' Eric asked.

'It's about the way you make a living, Mr Ward, dealing with low life. The first bit of bad news is that you've just lost a client.'

'A client? What do you mean?'

Charlie Spate's tone was edged with triumph. 'Joe Paulson. Forensic have found his body. So he won't be appearing in court next week, and I'm afraid you'll have lost your fees.'

Eric stared at him in surprise. Spate was pleased. 'You want the second piece of bad news now?'

Eric was going to get it whether he wanted it or not.

'It's about where we found Joe Paulson. The fact is, he was found dead up at Stagshaw. In that old, disused farmhouse outside the perimeter fence. He was a bit crisped up, but recognisable. But it was the farmhouse that was the seat of the fire, that ended with the explosion that ripped Stagshaw apart.'

Jackie Parton glanced at Eric. Spate intercepted the glance and his grin widened. 'So the third bit of bad news is that Paulson's death wasn't accidental, it was the result of an arson attack, and that means your other client, Eddie Ridout, is in deep trouble. If you're in touch with him, Ward, you'd better tell him to get his arse down here to Newcastle as fast as he can make it. Because he's right in the frame now—and the charge is likely to be murder!'

CHAPTER FOUR

1

Charlie Spate slumped in the chair in his office and winced at the recollection of the thudding in his skull as he had talked to the forensic pathologist at his tiny office in Gosforth. Elaine Start had taken him straight there—Charlie had been in no fit state to drive. She had asked him what was the reason for his pub crawl, and he really couldn't remember. It had started with a general feeling of depression, the idea that he was a fish out of water up here in the North, a reluctance to admit that he was feeling lonely: he had just pushed aside his desk work in the middle of the afternoon, and gone on a bender. The Northumberland Fusilier was only the last of the list before she found him. And when she had, and taken him to see the people at the forensic laboratory, he hadn't really been up to focussing on the matters in hand.

The little man with the moustache turned out to be called Paterson. He was aware of Charlie's state, and he rolled his eyes in Elaine Start's direction expressively. It was she who had asked the questions, mainly, while Charlie listened, partly to Paterson's replies, and partly to the growing noise in his head.

The forensic group had finally got around to taking a closer look at the deserted farmhouse. They had eventually reached the conclusion that it was on the ground floor, in the kitchen at the back, that the fire had been started. It had spread quickly, not least because it seemed as though there was a considerable amount of inflammable material there, paper, documents, and other items which had been liberally sprayed with petrol.

'If the intention was to blow up Stagshaw, why do you think the fire was started at the farmhouse?' Elaine Start had asked.

Paterson had gazed at her with a certain owlish admiration. Charlie had guessed the little man quite liked Elaine Start and had felt a stab of irritation. 'I didn't say an intention to affect Stagshaw was apparent from the evidence. And I'm not really qualified to look into motives. I just present facts.'

But it seemed that the fire had spread quickly in the old farmhouse, the rising wind had pushed flammable material into the compound beyond the perimeter fence where it had ignited chemicals on the site. Once ignition had occurred there, the fire had quickly spread throughout the Stagshaw site, culminating in a massive explosion. The explosion was one of the reasons why they had discovered the body, behind the damaged wall of the farmhouse. The wall had been blown down, the upper floor had collapsed, and the corpse had been thrown to the ground.

'The body had been badly burned, of course,' Paterson had explained, caressing his little moustache as though he thought it would be a turn on for Elaine Start. 'But it's not easy to burn a body unless the temperature is such that the flesh is consumed. In this case, the legs and torso had been badly damaged, but the head, oddly enough, was largely intact.'

'And you were able to identify the body as that of Joe Paulson.'

'Actually, from physical records supplied to us. He'd used a local dentist, and we quickly found a match for his teeth. The fact that we found his wallet, which included a note of a dental appointment, helped considerably in identifying him in the first instance.'

Charlie had hardly been able to believe it. It had all seemed so easy. 'Do you think that Paulson himself started the fire,' he had growled, 'and then got trapped in it?'

They had both stared at him as though he was demented. He didn't like the idea of Elaine Start and Dr Paterson ganging up on him.

'I said his head was largely untouched by the fire,' Paterson sneered. 'We found him outside the house, but it was clear he had fallen from the upstairs bedroom. And the side of his head had been heavily damaged.'

'By the fall?'

'By a blunt implement. Wielded at least two

or three times. The fact is, this man was murdered, in the upstairs room. Then, later, the fire was started down below.'

'By the murderer?' Elaine Start had asked.

The forensic pathologist was unwilling to contradict her, but shrugged. 'That I can't say. It's possible—it could have been an attempt to cover up the murder, destroy the evidence, so to speak. On the other hand, it's also possible that the person who started the fire never even knew that the dead man was there, upstairs. We'll be able to give a firmer view, in time, when we are able to settle more clearly on a time of death—because we know the time that the explosion took place. But at the moment . . .'

Which rather complicated things, in Charlie's view. What had seemed fairly clear-cut, was no longer quite so obvious.

And there was one other thing that bothered him. They had found Paulson's body at the site, but there was no vehicle nearby. So Paulson and the murderer must have arrived together—possibly in Paulson's car. After the killing, and the arson, the murderer had driven Paulson's car away. So where was it now? Perhaps, if they could find the vehicle, it might give them some clue to the identity of the killer.

He looked up as Elaine Start tapped on the door to his room. 'We'll be having the first one in the interview room in half an hour, sir. In

161

the meanwhile, I thought you'd better take a look at this.'

She handed him an envelope. He opened it and drew out several sheets of paper. The covering note, headed with the address of the forensic science laboratory, explained it was a list of the chemicals stored in drums at the site.

'The last sheet is actually a list provided by Stagshaw's site manager,' Elaine Start explained. 'I've already checked them out, compared the two lists. They match. With the exception of some items on the last sheet, the pink one you've got in your hand. There's certain items listed there—but no mention of them in the Stagshaw list.'

Charlie Spate stared at the sheet she had mentioned. Then he swore under his breath. He looked up. Elaine Start was staring at him, tight-lipped.

'*BSE-contaminated waste*?'

She nodded. 'I've already been in touch with the government laboratory at Gateshead. They were helpful. They explained that these solvents, contained in five-gallon drums, would have been used to wash infected cattle tissue samples. They agreed that the markings on the drums suggested they had originated from the Gateshead laboratory, but they insisted they had no record of them going to Stagshaw. The contract for destruction of the waste is with a firm in the West Country. They have no idea how the drums ended up at Stagshaw. The relevant documentation seems to have . . . disappeared.'

Charlie forgot all about the embarrassment of his throbbing skull. 'It seems to me that the site manager at Stagshaw has some explaining to do,' he said.

*   *   *

James Denton sat hugging himself in his chair in the interview room, arms crossed over his rotund little body. He was already sweating, Charlie was pleased to note, and there were shadows of uneasiness in his eyes. Charlie sat down in front of him, while Elaine Start stood a little to one side, observing. Charlie gave the Stagshaw site manager a foxy smile. 'We're not treating this in a formal way at the moment. Just wanted to have a chat with you. Clear up a few things, you know how it is.'

Denton nodded in relief. He managed a weak smile. 'I'll be glad to help in any way I can.'

'That's fine,' Charlie said heartily. 'Let's begin with the security arrangements at Stagshaw. The way they operated on the day of the explosion.'

Denton spoke hurriedly, in a flat monotone as though he was reciting a mantra. Perhaps it was like that: something he had practised for this moment, gone over time and again until it sounded convincing. It sounded unconvincing to Charlie. He listened patiently while the site manager explained that the watchman normally came on site ten minutes before the staff, including the security officer, left. But there had been occasions when there had been an 'interim', as he described it. This was one of them. The night watchman had been late. The staff had gone. The watchman had been delayed by the failure of his car to start. So he said. But he'd been late before. However, on this occasion it was perhaps as well he had been late, Denton suggested with a hint of brightness. Otherwise, he could have been injured in the blast.

'How late was he?' Charlie asked in an offhand tone.

Denton swallowed hard. 'About forty minutes, it seems. By a lucky chance.'

'Or by design.'

There was a short silence. At last, Denton said, 'I don't understand—'

Charlie picked up a pencil, began to play with it between his fingers. 'Well, maybe he'd been told to turn up late.'

'Who would do that?' Denton asked nervously. 'And why—'

'Well, let me put it this way. Maybe the person who started the fire that blew up Stagshaw suggested to the night watchman that it would be a good idea to stay away at that particular point in time.' Charlie paused, meaningfully. 'You have any thoughts about

164

that, Mr Denton?'

The site manager showed how he was flustered by flapping his hands helplessly, and twisting in his chair to send a look of appeal at Elaine Start. 'I've got no thoughts on it. I mean, I don't know what you're implying.'

'Well, let's talk about what was stored on site,' Charlie suggested. 'I have your list here. Industrial solvents, xylene, toluene, methylene chloride, mixed pesticides, and then there's trichlorethylene, cyanide . . . Anything else you can think of.'

There was a light sheen of sweat on Denton's forehead. He shook his head. 'The list I gave you, it covers all the stuff we'd been holding.'

'But the list doesn't mention any substances delivered from the Gateshead government laboratory.'

There was a long, pregnant silence. At last, Denton swallowed nervously. 'I . . . we don't have any dealings with the laboratory. Our contracts are with industrial—'

'So you've no idea how BSE-contaminated solvents came to be stored at Stagshaw?'

Denton's eyes were scared. 'I don't believe the suggestions you make are accurate.'

'You are the site manager, aren't you, Mr Denton?'

'Yes, of course, but . . .' Denton's eyes were suddenly panicked. 'I don't see how—'

'No,' Charlie interrupted in a steely tone,

165

'we don't see how, either. The information we have from the forensic lab is that it's clear at least three five-gallon drums of BSE-contaminated waste went up in that explosion. They found some of the drum materials burned out. But they also found another four drums, which did not go up in the big bang. In other words, there were at least seven drums of the stuff on site. Now how do you account for that, Mr Denton? You've agreed—you *are* the site manager. So isn't it your responsibility to know exactly what's going on at the site you manage? Did you know this stuff was on site? And if you didn't know . . . well, how the hell did it get there?'

Denton sat very still, struggling for breath. 'I . . . I don't know. And I thought we were going to be talking about how the explosion occurred. The matter of what was on site . . .'

'Well, things have got a bit complicated,' Charlie explained reasonably. 'You're probably aware that this has now turned into a murder enquiry. We thought at first no one had been killed in the explosion. But now we've found a corpse, so we have to broaden the scope of the enquiry. We would always have been looking for motivation—because it seems it was a case of arson, after all. We'd need to ask, who would want to blow up Stagshaw, and why?'

'The Ewart Village protest group, they had a motive,' Denton suggested weakly.

'Ha, yes, but we have to look elsewhere as

well, don't we? To make sure we're on the right track. And this particular track we're now on . . . I mean, BSE-contaminated waste! That would really get the protest group up in arms, wouldn't it? If they knew about it. But we've never heard of them complaining about that— as they surely would if they did hear about it! But how did it get there at Stagshaw? And why would somebody—a local manager, for instance—think it would be a good idea to torch Stagshaw? Maybe it was to get rid of the evidence.' Charlie paused, eyeing Denton carefully. 'When was your next site inspection due? Was it coming up soon? Wasn't there time to get rid of the waste before the inspectors came, and asked some very awkward questions? Such as where was your licence to store such waste materials? That sort of question, Mr Denton.'

There was a long silence. 'I don't think I want to continue with this interview,' Denton said at last, in a shaky tone. 'Not without having a solicitor present.'

'I can recommend a good one,' Charlie replied drily. 'Who happened to be at the scene just after the explosion. But unfortunately he's already acting for the protest group. And I think I can imagine what he's going to say when he hears about this latest development.'

*   *   *

167

The treatment was always going to be different for the owner of Stagshaw site. The Chief Constable had explained to Charlie that it was due to the serious and wider implications that the case had now assumed. So Lon Stanley would be invited to come to Ponteland merely for a discussion about those implications generally, at the office of the Chief Constable himself. And there would also be a representative of the Department of Environmental Health present. To keep a watching brief.

And to stop the proverbial hitting the fan, Charlie thought sourly. He wore his best suit to the meeting.

The civil servant was slim, middle-aged, pin-stripe suited, with thin lips and hawkish, predatory eyes. He introduced himself to Charlie in a typically civil service, public school manner. 'Palmer-Penrose,' he said extending his hand limply. His grip was cool, slightly damp-fleshed. Then he sat back, slightly to one side, as though distancing himself from the proceedings. Lon Stanley, big and confident, sat with folded arms while the Chief Constable opened the discussion.

'I thought it would be useful if we got together here, to discuss the implications of the situation, in an informal way, so that we could highlight the . . . ah . . . difficulties we are facing here. There are two main issues, of course. We have the discovery of the dead man—Paulson—at the farmhouse site, and the explosion at Stagshaw. Allied to these, naturally, is the question of what was actually stored on the site.'

Lon Stanley's hooded eyes flickered briefly, but he said nothing. The Chief Constable turned to Charlie Spate. 'Perhaps you'd like to outline our . . . concerns?'

Charlie nodded. 'To begin with, we're fairly clear how the explosion actually came about, and what happened to Paulson. We still have a number of enquiries to make, of course, but we're pretty sure that Paulson was murdered some little while before the fire was started. Flaming materials drifted onto the Stagshaw site, there was a consequent explosion, and . . . well, there we are. What we have to find out now, of course, is who was motivated to start this chain of events.'

'Do you know who owned the farmhouse?' Stanley asked sharply. 'It wasn't part of our holdings, so if you find out who owned the place maybe that'll point to the person who killed this Paulson man.'

Charlie shook his head. 'No, that won't help. You see, from our enquiries we've learned that the property was actually owned by Paulson himself.' Charlie paused, reflectively. 'Did you happen to know Paulson, Mr Stanley?'

'No.' The sharpness of the tone brooked no

169

discussion of the matter.

'I see.' Charlie allowed the silence to grow around them. The Chief Constable waited, shifting uncomfortably in his chair. At last Charlie, consulting his notes, said, 'Well, let's have a look at possible motives—'

'I would have thought there was no problem with motive,' Lon Stanley barked. 'We've had nothing but trouble from the protest group at the village, and then there's the matter of the threats Eddie Ridout made against me personally. I don't think you need to look further than him, as far as setting the fire was concerned. He couldn't get through our security—'

Charlie raised his eyebrows and Lon Stanley reddened. 'He couldn't get past our security,' he insisted, 'so he started the fire at the farmhouse, probably assisted its spread, and then got the hell out of there before the explosion took place.'

'And Paulson?'

There was a short silence. Stanley shrugged. 'Maybe Paulson caught him at it, and Ridout killed him. I don't know.'

'Neither do we, at this stage,' Charlie admitted. 'Because there's another problem there. If Ridout was firing the farmhouse, and Paulson caught him at it, there would be two cars at the site. But in fact, there were no cars discovered there at all. And then, well, there is another scenario we can put together.' Charlie

170

paused, eyeing Lon Stanley with an innocent air. 'You run a pretty tight ship, I am led to believe, Mr Stanley.'

The big man's mouth was hard. 'I make sure that all procedures are in place; I put in sound management; I keep an eye on them myself; I take a personal, hands-on approach to the business.'

'So I've been told,' Charlie said smoothly. 'And that's really why I'm so puzzled about the security arrangements—or lack of them—at Stagshaw.'

'Denton will be disciplined for any shortcomings identified in that area. It's his responsibility.'

'Yes, but you'd be hauling him over the coals rather late in the day. You see, Mr Stanley, I'm left with this curious thought. If you're so hands-on, if you're so much in control of your business and your managers, how come Denton was allowed to get away with such slackness in the first place?'

Stanley was silent, glaring at Charlie. The Chief Constable was watching the civil servant, Palmer—Penrose, who was sitting very still in his chair.

'Let me explain my thoughts out loud,' Charlie suggested. 'Maybe this was all a matter of slackness by Denton. Maybe it was an oversight on your part. But I have to look at things from all sides. Maybe it wasn't slackness: maybe the whole thing was set up

171

deliberately.'

Stanley opened his mouth to say something, but thought better of it.

'You see,' Charlie continued, 'it could have been that Denton deliberately told his security people to stay away He closed the site down. Made sure there was no one around. Because he knew something was going to happen.'

'Denton wouldn't have had the—'

'Guts?' Charlie smiled. 'Then maybe he was told to do it.'

Stanley wanted to move to the offensive, knowing what was behind Charlie's remark. But he steeled himself to remain silent. Palmer-Penrose leaned forward slightly, his sharp eyes glinting. 'That . . . er . . . comment would seem to suggest that Mr Denton, or some other person in authority, would have reason to cause an explosion at Stagshaw. Which is bringing you around, I imagine, to consider the reasons why such an explosion would be desirable. And that is designed to bring my department into consideration.'

Charlie was pleased with himself. 'Well, you might say that, Mr Palmer-Penrose. We would certainly like to know what's been going on. One view of the facts might be that Mr Stanley ordered Denton to keep his security man away—' Charlie ignored the protest that came from Stanley, and from the Chief Constable's struggling upright, warningly, in his chair. 'But why would that be, unless it was in Mr

Stanley's interests, or Mr Denton's interests if you like, to destroy materials at Stagshaw?'

'You're referring, of course, to the BSE-contaminated waste,' Palmer-Penrose said coldly. 'I think we are all aware that Stagshaw held no licence to store or incinerate such waste products. But I also have to give you this assurance. The matter has now been investigated thoroughly in my department. I have personally checked with the local and regional office. Seventeen drums of such waste at Gateshead were dealt with in the proper manner, and were incinerated. The firm that had the responsibility for this action is based in Exeter. Quite how the drums then came to be at the Stagshaw site is a matter for astonishment on our part. Certainly, we can take no responsibility for the presence of the drums.'

'So,' Charlie purred, 'you can take no responsibility even though it is the department's responsibility to see to it that such waste is properly disposed of. That must mean that there will be matching documentation held by the Exeter company, and by your regional office, which will show that the drums were despatched from Gateshead and received in Exeter, and then it follows that the Exeter company will have documentation regarding its incineration.'

Coolly, Palmer-Penrose said, 'Government records are of course confidential.'

173

'But would have to be produced under subpoena.'

'We don't maintain records over a significant period—'

'What's that, six months, two years?'

Palmer-Penrose's gaze was calm, and his appearance unruffled. 'I fail to see what you're trying to show, DCI Spate.'

Charlie glanced at the Chief Constable. He shrugged. 'All big organisations have problems with paperwork from time to time. But government departments, staffed by civil servants, well, we expect their records would be immaculate. Yet I'm left with the feeling that maybe your regional office can't produce the relevant documentation, any more than Mr Stanley here can show us a licence that permits Stagshaw to handle such contaminated waste. So I have to wonder, what the hell is going on?'

Palmer-Penrose smiled thinly. His eyes were cold. 'First of all, if I may make a comment as a layman unaccustomed to police procedures, it seems to me that you are failing to concentrate on the important issues here.'

'Which are?' Charlie growled, annoyed at the civil servant's patronising tone.

'How this man Paulson was killed, and by whom. The matter of records regarding the disposal of waste, of whether or not licences were issued to the site to carry this kind of waste, these are side issues as far as you're

174

concerned. They properly belong to checks and investigations that should be carried out within my department. So, I would advise a concentration only on the issues important to you, DCI Spate. Naturally, my department will be only too happy to help over the matter of licences and records—when we feel that they are issues of importance that need to be addressed. But we do not need . . . others, to tell us how to maintain our administration.' He smiled coldly in the direction of the Chief Constable. 'I think that now I am clear concerning the major issues, I had better leave. I have other business to attend to, but I will, naturally, be at your service any time you wish to call to see me at headquarters.'

He rose, nodded, and left the room. There was a short silence. Lon Stanley heaved himself to his feet. 'And I think that does for me too. I resent the way in which you've been suggesting—'

'Mr Stanley,' Charlie interrupted, 'just one more moment. How's your financial situation?'

Stanley glared at him. 'What the hell's that got to do with you?'

'You say you didn't know Paulson?'

'What are you getting at?'

'Paulson was a grubber, a turner-up of information, a seeker-out of scandal. He died in an old farmhouse adjoining your property. Stagshaw goes up in flames. You'll have big insurance cover, of course. Maybe that's why you told Denton to keep the watchman away that day.'

'I don't have to listen to this,' Stanley snarled in a fury that might have been assumed. 'Chief Constable, this was supposed to be an informal meeting. I didn't come here to be accused and insulted. If you want to see me again, talk to my lawyer.'

The door slammed behind him. The Chief Constable remained seated in his chair, staring at Charlie with barely concealed dislike. 'You came here from the Met with a reputation.'

'Not for handling villains with kid gloves, sir,' Charlie replied truculently.

'What the hell did you expect to get out of that kind of behaviour?' the Chief Constable growled. 'Throwing wild accusations around—'

'Maybe not so wild,' Charlie insisted. 'Oh, Stanley would love us to concentrate on Eddie Ridout—and he's still not out of my frame, sir—but that doesn't mean we should ignore the other possibilities. Paulson was a mud-grubber. He made a lot of enemies. I think we should look into the finances of Lon Stanley; we should find out whether there was any money exchanging hands between Denton and the government laboratory staff at Gateshead; we should find out just what control Stanley does have over his staff. I don't want to be led by the nose by people like Palmer-Penrose, who I'm sure as hell is fully aware that

176

government regulations have been flouted by his own staff, that his records are either non-existent or faulty, or that his staff have been up to some fiddles or other with the bypassing of the Exeter waste disposal firm.'

'Have you got evidence of any of this?' the Chief Constable queried.

Charlie shook his head. 'I'm just laying down some hypotheses,' he insisted.

'*Hypotheses*, is it? Is that what they call it in the Met?' The Chief Constable grunted contemptuously. 'At least it gets you away from your obsession with Jack Tenby.'

Charlie raised his head like a wolf sniffing the wind. 'Far from it, sir. I told you—Paulson gathered dirt on everyone. I wouldn't be surprised if he had some on Mad Jack Tenby— maybe on drugs, maybe on whores. The fire at Stagshaw may have been accidental, or maybe not. But Paulson's dead, and his killing is central to it all. But that doesn't leave my obsession, as you call it, outside the window.'

'I think it's time, DCI,' the Chief Constable suggested, 'you started uncluttering your mind.'

And deep down, Charlie had to agree with him.

2

The valley had been formed by a geological fault and carved and smoothed by the action of glaciers. Eric drove the Celica along the single-track, rutted road for just over a mile, then pulled in at the side and parked on a grassy bank that looked down on Hawsen Burn. The valley floor was sheep-grazed, unimproved because of the regular flooding of Harthope Burn: along the terraces carved by the stream gorse grew in thick clumps, glowing yellow, and willow scrub dotted the slopes.

A half mile further on was the ice-sculpted ravine and beyond that the steep-sided gorge watered by a rushing burn that cascaded over small waterfalls, shouldered by crags and scree where patches of alpine vegetation survived. It was a wild and lonely place, but beautiful, half-hidden by the shoulder of the crag but overlooking the lonely valley that ran deep into the heart of the Cheviots.

Eric saw the Land Rover first, and beyond it the tent. It was pitched on a flat-topped hummock on the bank side, sheltered by a copse of tall beech trees. There was no one there, so Eric walked on past the tent and the vehicle towards the glade below, leading down to the burn. It was there that he found Eddie Ridout. He was seated on a decayed, fallen log, staring out over the valley, shoulders hunched, hands thrust deep into the pockets of his waxy jacket. He must have heard Eric's approach, even above the subdued murmuring of the stream but he did not look up until Eric stood beside him.

'Mr Ward.' His tone was marked with indifference. He seemed neither surprised, nor disturbed to see Eric.

'People have been wondering where you'd got to.'

Eddie Ridout picked up a small pebble at his feet and tossed it absent-mindedly into the stream. 'I used to bring Sam up here when he was a kid,' he said. 'He loved it. There was always rabbits, and the odd pheasant, though in the end he wasn't much interested in shooting. Except crows. We used to go crow-shooting at dusk, around the farm. And the burn here, there's some deep pools down beyond that bend where it's so peaceful you could imagine you had reached the end of the world. We used to come up here, pitch our tent, fish and dream. It was a grand time. It changed, of course: after his mother died there was a period when Sam wanted to be up here most weekends, but by himself. I understood that. It's not that he blamed me for her death in any way—it was that he felt let down somehow, by the fact she was gone. Maybe he didn't want to get too close with me any more: too much to lose. It didn't matter. A few years later, we were back, good mates again— though not so much coming up here together. There was the farm to look after, and he enjoyed it. And then one day he complained about a burning sensation on his upper lip. That's when it started . . .'

He was silent for a little while. Then he looked up at Eric curiously. 'How did you find me?'

Eric looked about him, at the valley, the burn, the wooded slopes in the near distance. 'I asked someone to make enquiries. There were some farmers he knew. One of them told him you used to come up here with Sam often, when he was a lad. I got directions.'

Ridout grimaced. 'Aye, well, sitting up here this last week has straightened out some of my feelings.' He paused, shook his head slowly. 'I don't want to be involved any more, Mr Ward. With Sam gone, I just don't see any point in going on. At first, like, it was the anger, the fury, the determination to get something done. But now, it all seems to be irrelevant. Even the farm. I'll have to sell it. Move away. Too many memories.'

Eric stepped over the end of the log and sat down beside him. Quietly, he said, 'It's not going to be that simple, Mr Ridout.'

'Why? There's nothing to hold me to Ewart now.'

'The police are looking for you.'

Ridout was still for a moment, then his head turned slowly so that he was staring at Eric. 'The police? What do they want?'

Eric hesitated. 'You know that Stagshaw went up in flames?'

If Eddie Ridout was surprised, he made no show of it. 'I'd be a hypocrite if I said I was sorry.'

'The police want to talk to you about it.'

Ridout frowned. 'How can I help them?'

'The day the explosion took place, I'd been to my home at Sedleigh Hall, but decided to call to see you, on the way back to Newcastle. But when I got there, you weren't at your farm. And then I heard the explosion. I went down to the site. Where were you that day, Mr Ridout?'

'I don't even know what day you're talking about,' Ridout muttered evasively. 'Couple of days after the funeral I couldn't stand it any longer, around the farm. Everything seemed cold, and empty And at last I thought about Harthope Valley. So I threw some things into a bag, packed the tent and came up here. Been here ever since: haven't seen a soul.'

There was a false note in his voice that puzzled Eric. He was holding something back, Eric was certain. He thought about it, waiting, but when Ridout remained silent, Eric leaned forward. 'What day exactly was it, that you came up here?'

Ridout squinted up at the pale blue sky and shrugged. 'Thursday, I suppose. After the funeral the house seemed . . . empty.'

'What time of day did you leave the farm?'

Reluctantly, Ridout admitted, 'Late afternoon. What's all these questions for? Does it matter what time I came up here?'

'It was just after five-thirty on the Thursday

181

that the fire and explosion at Stagshaw took place. Did you know nothing about it?'

There was an uneasy silence. 'I been up here for days,' Ridout muttered in a non-committal tone.

The silence lengthened about them. Something splashed lightly in the stream below them, and a buzzard soared high above their heads, using the thermals to climb, circling watching for prey. A light breeze rose, whispering among the willow trees clustered near the bank. 'You went down there, didn't you Eddie?' Eric said quietly.

It was some time before Ridout answered. Then he sighed, ran a gnarled hand over his stubbled face. He nodded. 'Aye, I went down there. I don't know what it was really. After the funeral I was restless. I felt confused, angry, uncertain what to do. I don't think I had anything in particular in mind. I wanted to do something, for sure. Tear the place down. I don't know. And I sat on the hill above Stagshaw and I stared down at it, and I thought of Sam and the waste of it all. If I'd have been able to get my hands around Lon Stanley's throat at that point, I think I'd have strangled him.'

'So what did you do?'

'Do?' Ridout seemed puzzled. 'I didn't do anything. Like I said, it all came to me that it was a waste of time, nothing really mattered much any more. Sam was gone: nothing could

182

bring him back. What was the point of pushing further? So I left. Got back in the Land Rover. Came up here.'

Carefully, Eric suggested, 'But you did know about Stagshaw.'

Ridout's fingernails rasped on his beard stubble, scratching uneasily. He nodded, grimacing with reluctance. 'I was driving up the hill when I saw the smoke. I stopped, looked back, and I have to admit when I heard the explosion a little later I felt a sense of relief. But it was nothing to do with me: I felt disconnected, somehow. If the place went up, I didn't care. If nothing happened to Stagshaw, I didn't care about that either. It was all in the past, I had to sort out my mind, and my life. In the end we all have to look to the future, Mr Ward, even if there's nothing to look forward to.'

'The police think you might have been responsible for the explosion,' Eric said.

Ridout gave a short, barking laugh. 'If I'd have thought of it, if I'd have had dynamite, maybe I'd have done it. But since Sam died I've been good for nothing, Mr Ward. My mind's been going round in circles. Can't fix to anything. Not even blowing up Stanley's waste dump.'

'But why did you go there at all that day?' Eric persisted.

Ridout frowned in thought. 'I don't know. I was confused. I wanted to do something, get back at Stanley. And maybe if no one had been around, who knows? Maybe I'd have tried *something*. But what? I didn't know what to do.'

Eric thought for a moment. 'There were people still on the site when you left?'

Ridout shook his head. 'No. I saw them leave. The site was deserted: they'd all knocked off.'

'But a moment ago, you said if no one had been around . . .'

'Yeah, of course. But they weren't on site. What I mean is, I saw the workers leave, and maybe I was still trying to think of some way of getting at Stanley, and maybe there was some crazy idea that I'd break into the site, climb the fence, do some damage, that sort of thing. But when I saw the cars, well, I just turned away.'

'Cars?' Eric asked, puzzled. 'What cars are you talking about?'

'There were two cars, parked outside the perimeter fence. Funny, really: I mean, that farmhouse was deserted, I always understood. But that afternoon, there were two cars parked at the side of the farm, away from the fence, sort of hidden from Stagshaw by the house itself. Anyway, I thought if there was someone there, they'd be able to see me breaking in, and I didn't know what I wanted to do anyway, so I just left . . .' He hesitated. 'I did sort of hear a muffled thump, later, when I was

184

driving up on the fell. That would have been the dump going up. But I didn't want to know. I'd washed my hands of it. I'd had enough of Stagshaw.'

Eric was silent for a while, thinking. 'These two cars . . . what do you think was going on at the farm?'

Ridout shrugged carelessly. 'No idea. Wasn't interested.'

'Did you see the owners? I mean, were they talking together outside, or were they inside the house?'

Ridout shook his head. His eyes clouded slowly as he thought back. 'No . . . but there was something that struck me as odd. I saw the cars there from the hill, and then I went back to the Land Rover. But when I was getting in I saw someone come around from the back of the house. He was moving in an odd way.'

'How do you mean?'

Ridout sucked his teeth in thought. 'He was . . . crouching like. He scuttled up to one of the cars and got in. Looked like he was about to drive away. And that's what I thought was odd.'

'How do you mean?'

Ridout turned to face him, eyes hazy with memory. 'He was just a kid. Small, wiry. Of course, I've seen youngsters driving tractors on farms when they're under age, but this kid didn't look like a farm lad to me. Can't tell you why . . .'

Eric took a deep breath. 'I think you'd better pack up now, Mr Ridout. We need to get to Newcastle, to see the police, before they come looking for you up here.'

*   *   *

Eric could tell that Charlie Spate didn't believe it.

He leaned back in his chair in the interview room, staring in veiled hostility at Eddie Ridout. His glance slipped towards Eric, and then back again to the farmer. 'So let's get this clear,' he suggested coldly, 'you admit you went down there late on that Thursday afternoon; you admit you wanted to do injury to Stanley—'

'My client didn't exactly say that,' Eric interrupted.

'I know what he said! He said he went there, had some thoughts of revenge, but didn't do anything. And didn't know about the fire—except he did see some smoke, and didn't know about the explosion—except he did hear a bang, and decided to go sleeping in the woods without wondering what was going on, or what might have happened, or who might have been injured—'

'My client's mind has been in a disturbed state, Mr Spate.'

'I'll say *disturbed*,' Charlie Spate sneered. 'And now he says he saw cars at the farmhouse.

186

What make were these cars?'

Ridout shrugged indifferently. 'I didn't pay that much attention.'

'Colour?'

'They were both dark coloured, that's all I can say.'

'And you saw a boy enter one of them. Did you see him drive away?'

Ridout shook his head. 'Not actually drive away. But he got in, sort of ducked down behind the dashboard. Then I left.'

'Ducked down?' Spate leaned forward. 'What, like he was trying to hide? Or was trying to hotwire the car? Did he look as if he was trying to steal the vehicle?'

Ridout shook his head. 'I don't know. Like I said, I left.'

'And can you describe the boy?'

'Not really. It was too far away. I just saw he was small, quick. That's all.'

Charlie Spate clearly thought it was not enough. He went over it all again with Ridout, but the answers he received were the same. Eric was aware of Spate's frustration, but he felt that it was partly due to the fact that Spate himself was beginning to feel Ridout's answers rang true. Even if he was unwilling to admit it.

After another half an hour, Spate gave up. He rose to his feet. 'All right, Mr Ridout. I'd like you to make a written statement. No doubt you'll want to supervise the activity, Mr Ward.' His cold eyes settled meaningfully on

187

Eric. 'Make sure your client doesn't stumble over anything. Then, perhaps you'd be good enough to give me a few minutes of your time.'

Half an hour later, Eric tapped on the door of Charlie Spate's office and when he entered was offered a chair. DCI Spate had a pile of folders in front of him: he pushed them aside now and stared at Eric. He seemed more relaxed than when he had been questioning Eddie Ridout.

'So, what's the latest on the protest group, Mr Ward? Where do they stand now?'

'In a much stronger position,' Eric replied evenly. 'I think Lon Stanley will have to settle pretty quickly: I'm sure his lawyers will advise him he doesn't stand much chance if matters go to court.'

'Because of the explosion?'

Eric nodded. 'There's a leading case—*Rylands v Fletcher*—which established that if dangerous substances are held on land, and those substances escape, causing damage, the person using the land will be responsible. There were dangerous substances held at Stagshaw; there was an explosion; there was an escape of noxious fumes. Stanley's liable.'

'Even if the explosion was caused by someone else?'

Eric nodded. 'Makes no difference. The matter of who is liable is indisputable. The explosion took place. There was an escape of dangerous matter. That's all that has to be proved. The land user is liable. The only question to be answered then is how much damages he'll have to pay.'

'And what if Stanley himself arranged the explosion?'

Eric's eyes widened. 'Then it's a matter for you—as well as damages for the villagers. But are you suggesting—'

Charlie Spate waved the question aside. 'I got an open mind. We'll see. But why didn't the villagers use this argument after the other explosions over the last few years?'

'They weren't advised by a good lawyer,' Eric replied coolly.

Charlie Spate grinned. 'Maybe that's right. And Ridout, he's got a good lawyer now, when he needs one.' He eyed Eric mockingly. 'You lawyers don't have to believe their clients are innocent, that's right?'

Impassively, Eric said, 'We merely present the case for our clients. Our own views are really irrelevant.'

'But I get the impression you really do believe Ridout's story.' Charlie Spate grunted, rose from behind his desk and began to pace around the room, his head lowered in thought. 'And if he did see a kid enter that car, maybe that explains something, at least . . . That guy I saw you with the other day. In the Northumberland Fusilier.'

'Jackie Parton?'

'That's him. The ex-jockey. He any good?'

189

Eric paused. 'He knows Tyneside.'

'So I gather . . . Anyway, let's talk about your ex-client Paulson. He got clobbered in that farmhouse. You have any idea what he was doing there?'

Eric shook his head.

'He owned it, you know.' Charlie Spate stopped pacing, stood behind his desk and fixed a penetrating glance on Eric. 'Like he owned a place off Fenhall Hall Drive. You knew about that place, is my guess.'

Eric hesitated, then nodded. 'He took me there.'

'It would've helped if you'd mentioned that to us. But no matter. We looked the place over. Full of paper, documents. Nothing important—few bits of scandal, and we've still got officers sifting through it, just in case. But the place where Paulson died . . . the farmhouse. Forensic tell us that there was a lot of paper stored there as well. It mostly went up in the flames. Fact is, we wonder whether that was why the place got torched in the first place.'

He watched Eric carefully. When there was no comment, he went on, 'You see we have to follow all sort of lines of enquiry. First, there's Lon Stanley and his manager Denton: what were they up to? I won't bore you with the details, but I've got them in the frame. And then there's your client Ridout: I don't rule him out, in spite of what he says. Where's the corroboration? And then there's what Paulson was storing in the farmhouse. Maybe that was why he was killed—and maybe the explosion at Stagshaw was just an accident. Who knows, at this stage? One fact is central, even so—a lot of people could have wanted your ex-client Paulson dead.'

'Because of his nocturnal activities,' Eric said flatly.

Charlie Spate nodded. 'Believe it. Let's take some suppositions. Suppose James Denton had some fiddle going at that waste site and Paulson found documentation about it. Suppose Stanley had ordered, or knew about the fiddle. Suppose one or the other got rid of two birds with one stone: knock off Paulson—who was blackmailing them—and torch the evidence, and Stagshaw itself. Although the Stagshaw burning could still have been accidental, of course. Never mind.' He pushed his chair back, slumped down into it. 'And then there's various others around who might have wanted Paulson knocked on the head. Let's take one example. Someone like, for instance Mad Jack Tenby . . .'

'You think he's involved?' Eric asked in surprise.

'I didn't say so. But, he's involved in prostitution, drugs, maybe your client had paper on him too.'

'The list will be long,' Eric suggested quietly. 'Joe Paulson was about to be hauled into

191

court, and he was more than annoyed that people he thought should have supported him weren't prepared to do so. There were politicians, businessmen, newspaper editors . . .'

'Who'll be sleeping safer in their beds once they know his cache of documentary goodies has gone up in smoke.'

Eric was about to say something, but bit back the words. 'Why exactly are you discussing all this with me?'

Charlie Spate took a deep breath. 'Well, let's say I regard you as a mucker.' He laughed shortly at the expression on Eric's face. 'Well, all right, if not a bosom friend, at least someone who has interests in common with me. And who owes me one.'

'What is it you want?' Eric asked slowly.

Charlie Spate shrugged. 'A bit of assistance. We've got our own people on the street, of course, but a grass can be very unreliable. He'll tell you what he thinks you want to hear, rather than the truth. But this guy you use . . . Jackie Parton . . . maybe he'd be different. Maybe he'll come up with some straight information, if he's working for you, rather than me.'

'I don't know about that . . .' Eric said reluctantly.

'Just get him to ask around,' Spate cut in, a hint of steel in his voice. 'That's all I ask. Find out what the vibrations are, humming off Paulson's killing. Who's nervous. Who's happy.

And then there's the boy.'

'The one Eddie Ridout saw?'

Charlie Spate nodded. There was a thoughtful haze in his eyes. 'You ever hear of a kid the newspapers call Batboy?'

Eric nodded. 'Terry Bell.'

'Ask Jackie Parton what he knows about him, as well. What he's been up to. I just have a gut feeling . . .'

Both men were silent for a while. Eric was uneasy at the thought of asking Parton to do some digging for the police: working for Eric was one thing, acting as a police informer was another. He looked up, caught DCI Spate's glance. It was hard, and calculating. 'I'd regard it as a favour, Mr Ward.'

Eric rose to go, without making any commitment. He reached the door, and stopped. Spate was watching him, expectantly.

'You said there are people who could sleep more easily now that the farmhouse—and its contents have gone up in smoke.'

'That's right.'

'Pandoras, Paulson called them.'

Spate frowned, puzzled. 'What's that supposed to mean?'

'Places where he kept the documentation he'd gathered over the years, from his rooting around at night in skips, waste bins, rubbish collections outside offices. He called them his Pandora boxes. You know the story of Pandora, Mr Spate: she opened up the box, out of curiosity, and all the evils of the world flew out.'

'Joe Paulson had a sense of humour, then.' Charlie Spate shrugged. 'So?'

'The house in Fenham was a Pandora. From what you tell me, it looks as though the farmhouse also was one of his Pandoras.'

Charlie Spate raised his eyebrows. 'So it would seem. What's your point?'

'I thought you ought to know,' Eric replied. 'Joe Paulson told me he had *three* Pandora boxes. I wonder where the other one might be?'

3

It had been as Eric had feared. When he had arranged a meeting with Jackie Parton, the ex-jockey had not been at all pleased at the suggestion made to him. He had outlined grimly where the distinction lay: it was one thing working for a lawyer, using his contacts to bring information which might be of assistance to Eric Ward's clients. It was quite another doing what he called the 'polis dirty work' for them.

'It's a matter of degree, maybe that's the way you see it, Mr Ward. But for me it's more than that. I'm well known along the river and I'm trusted. This would be too much like grassing—and my reputation would be damaged if it got out. Once that happens, my contacts disappear and I might even end up in an alley in a more than bruised state myself. I'm sorry, Mr Ward, but it's not on.' He had eyed Eric carefully. 'Whatever pressure DCI Spate might be applying.'

Eric knew that the ex-jockey was aware that Spate had some sort of unsettled debt due to him, but he was disinclined to respond to Jackie Parton's comment. He considered the matter carefully, and at last he had been forced to agree with Parton.

'I take your point. But can we do it this way? I still have Ridout as a client and he's still under suspicion for Paulson's murder. So I have an interest in getting any information that will assist in clearing Ridout. The fact that the information might be helpful to Spate is irrelevant.'

'And I don't need to know whether you feed any of it to Spate, or not,' Jackie Parton growled. He still seemed doubtful, but Eric guessed he would be coming around. 'I suppose, if we regard it as between you and me . . .' His voice had trailed away uncertainly 'Well, what is it you want anyway?'

'The talk along the river. About Paulson. About his activities. About who was particularly nervous in the context of his nightly activity: Lon Stanley; his manager Denton; Jack Tenby.'

'Mad Jack?' The ex-jockey shook his head ruefully. 'If Paulson had crossed Mad Jack, it could well have ended with his head bashed in.'

'And find out what you can about Terry Bell.'

'The Batboy?' Jackie Parton had been curious. 'Where does that little scallywag fit into this?'

Eric had explained that he wasn't sure, and that he raised the name merely because Eddie Ridout claimed to have seen a boy up at Stagshaw before the explosion occurred. He did not mention Charlie Spate's 'gut feeling'. Jackie Parton had shaken his head. 'Naw, Terry bell, he's a twocker and a thief, but arson's not his style at all. Still, I'll ask around, like. Might come up with something.'

*   *   *

And now, in the late afternoon several days later, Jackie Parton had rung Eric at his office. It was time they had another chat. Eric fixed the time for six o'clock, at the Northumberland Fusilier. Then he settled down to clear his desk of some paperwork. After a while, he walked out into the anteroom where his secretary worked.

Susie Cartwright was looking at the early evening edition of the newspaper. He knew she had made some small investments in shares, and checked them every day. He'd gained the impression she regarded herself as

196

really rather shrewd as far as stocks and shares were concerned.

'So, you made your million yet, Susan?'

She laughed. 'Fat chance, with the amounts I have. But they're holding up in spite of the rollercoaster ride the index has been suffering lately. Still, it's just as well I didn't put some money into the Holystone Mining that I mentioned the other day.'

'Why's that?'

'Looks like there's going to be a Stock Exchange investigation into the rights issues. And into the share prices of Sandhurst Securities. Now that would hardly have done this firm's reputation any good would it, Mr Ward? Your secretary getting involved in dodgy share issues.'

'I've got enough problems as it is, Susie,' Eric groaned in agreement. 'One of them is cash flow. Have we had the bills back from the costs draftsman yet?'

She shook her head. 'I'll get on to them immediately, Mr Ward. By the way, I've fixed another appointment for you this afternoon. A Mr Preece.' She saw the grimace he made, and asked hurriedly, 'Should I cancel it?'

After a moment, Eric shook his head. 'No, I'll see him. But it's not going to help your salary. I don't think he'll be wanting to enlist our services as a legal representative.'

*   *   *

Eric was right in his guess. Karl Preece arrived an hour later and settled into the chair in front of Eric's desk.

'And what can I do for the gentlemen of the Press?' Eric asked ironically.

'Provide information, what else?' Preece grinned.

'If you're wanting to know whether I've found out anything regarding the *Princess Eugenie* business, the answer is in the negative.'

'The Jason Sullivan thing?' Preece shook his head. 'No, I didn't come about that. It's still rumbling on, and maybe I'll tell you about that later. No, it's really about Joe Paulson. As you know, I run a financial column in the weekend nationals, but Paulson is reputed to have had information on various financial firms so I was thinking of doing a piece on him. You know— *Lurking Timebombs For Flaky Financial Houses.* Something catchy like that. I think I can get the right sort of piece syndicated. I knew you were representing him, at the hearing. But now he's dead, I just wondered whether there's anything you can tell me about it.'

'Now what makes you think I'd have any information for you?'

Preece shrugged, spread his hands wide. 'Come on, Mr Ward! Give me a break. You have no need to hide Joe Paulson's secrets

198

now—the nightwalker's dead, and the great unwashed public are screaming to know all about it. And surely you're the one who can help—after all, not only did you represent the dead man, but you're also acting on behalf of one of the persons suspected of the murder.'

Eric stared at the newspaperman silently.

'You know,' Preece urged after a moment. 'Eddie Ridout.'

Eric thought the matter over for a little while, as Preece waited expectantly. Carefully, he said, 'My client Eddie Ridout has been interviewed by the police. No charges have been made, and as far as I'm aware at the moment, no charges are contemplated.'

'That's not the way I heard it.'

'I can't be responsible for what unfounded gossip you might have picked up.'

'Unfounded, well, maybe, maybe not.' Karl Preece cocked his head on one side like an inquisitive blackbird. 'But, you know, there are as many leaks from the local nick as there are from anywhere else.'

Eric knew it, thinking back to the old days when he had been on the beat. There were always loose mouths, or greedy hands, prepared to release snippets of information to the newspapers. He shrugged indifferently. 'Then you'd better pick up what you can from those sources.'

'You're not being very helpful, Mr Ward. Remember, anything you might give me, well,

199

it could be of assistance to your client.'

'Such as?'

Preece pursed his lips. 'Well, you say your client Ridout isn't being charged. But is there anyone else the police are looking at? Are there any other leads you think they might be following? I've got contacts. I could be useful. Give me some names, maybe I'll come up with something.'

It would be supping with the devil, Eric knew it. Using Preece could be a mistake, but the man was a reporter, and would have his own underworld contacts. There was the possibility he could use sources that would be able to confirm whatever Jackie Parton came up with. Eric had no illusions about Preece's offer to help, but at the same time it might be worth giving the reporter something to work on.

'Anything I say will have to be off the record,' he commented slowly.

Preece grinned in triumph. 'You got my absolute guarantee, Mr Ward.'

'There's little I can say that you haven't already got, or will find out shortly, I've no doubt. But, first, Paulson died before the farmhouse was set on fire. It's possible that the fire was started in order to destroy documentation held there—'

'Documentation?'

Eric smiled wryly. 'Come on, you know what Paulson was up to night after night. You denied to me you ever used any of his stuff, but you must have realised he had a great deal of it stashed away somewhere. Well, it seems the old farmhouse was one of his little hideaways.'

'One of them?'

'He had others. A house near Fenham Hall Drive, for instance.'

'The police have looked the place over?' Preece asked.

Eric nodded. 'They've removed a fair bit of paper. Still checking through it, I understand.'

Preece raised his head like a questing, eager hound. 'And as a result, they're beginning to look at certain people?'

Eric hesitated. Reluctantly, he said, 'Well, yes, I suppose so. And for other reasons too. Paulson's activities made a lot of enemies.'

'And is there any connection between Paulson's killing, and the Stagshaw explosion?'

'Who knows at this stage? It could have been accidental.'

'But Lon Stanley's been down to be interviewed, I hear.' Preece grinned wolfishly. 'And the site manager. But was it over the explosion, or over Paulson's death?'

'I can't say,' Eric replied coldly. 'The police don't confide in me.'

'But Paulson must have done. And what's Ridout's story? I've spoken to him, by the way, but all he told me was something about seeing a boy up there.'

That had been a mistake. Eric should have warned Ridout to say nothing to the Press. 'I'm sorry. I'm unable to confirm or deny anything Mr Ridout might have told you in confidence.'

'Yeah, of course. Client privilege and all that.' Preece leaned back looking disappointed. 'It's just that Ridout told me he thought you might be looking for the kid. To confirm Ridout's story.' He waited, but when Eric remained silent, he went on, 'Okay, so there's Stanley and the site manager, but who else?'

Eric hesitated. He thought back to his conversation with Charlie Spate. 'I think,' he said hesitantly,' the police will also be looking at certain . . . underworld figures.'

Preece stared at him. 'Paulson's death could have been a gang killing?' He pursed his lips in a silent whistle. 'I suppose it makes sense. There's a few along the Tyne . . . like Mad Jack Tenby.' When Eric made no confirmatory reply, Preece sighed. 'Well, I'll see what I can dredge up. It's a living, after all. Now, about that *Princess Eugenie* thing.'

'I told you. I've no more information—'

'But I have.'

There was a short silence. Preece kept him waiting. It was a payback for his own reluctance to divulge information. 'There's still nothing that can be confirmed in writing,' he said at last, 'but from my sources I hear that

202

the Fraud Squad have now been given information regarding the transhipping of the cargo from the *Princess Eugenie*. It seems that it's now confirmed that the denim finally turned up back in Turkey. And that means the insurers will turn down the claim arising from the loss of the *Princess Eugenie*. They're going to argue that the risk under the contract never attached, since the voyage contemplated under the bill of lading never took place.'

'That would seem to follow. And it's a response one would expect from the insurers.'

Preece watched him for a few moments with a conspiratorial air. 'But where does that leave your friend Sullivan?'

Eric was inclined to deny the friendship but made no reply.

'It seems that he's got to attend a hearing before the Benchers of his Inn. Now it's not to be a formal hearing, it's all a bit hush-hush, but concerns raised by the financial houses are putting pressure on the Benchers. Maybe he'll get away with his knuckles rapped.'

'Or maybe he can show he's done nothing wrong,' Eric suggested.

'Ah, well, there you are. But smoke and fire, Mr Ward! All I would say is, better warn your wife that she'd be better advised getting someone else to represent her interests in Martin and Channing. Sullivan could come out of this business somewhat stained, you know what I mean. So I should have a word in her shell-like, as they say'

It was one piece of advice Eric would not be taking.

*   *   *

The lounge bar of the Northumberland Fusilier was rather more crowded than it had been on the occasion of Eric's last meeting with Jackie Parton. Eric had had a problem parking the Celica, but had managed to squeeze it in at the parking area behind the pub. The ex-jockey was a little late so Eric got himself a drink and made his way over to a small corner table just across from a group of raucous, scantily-dressed young women who were clearly out to celebrate something or other. A few comments were passed, and some heads turned to look at him before fits of giggles swept the group, but they soon lost interest in him and continued their inanities in loud, juvenile voices.

When Jackie Parton finally arrived he raised his eyebrows at the sight of the girls. One of them turned, caught sight of him and whooped. 'Wey, hey, bonny lad! How are you, Jackie man? You got somewhere to park your bandy little legs tonight, then?'

'Not at your place,' he retorted, grinning. 'Yer mam might find out!'

He sat down beside Eric and grimaced. 'And I'm right serious, too. That lass is young enough to be me daughter.'

He refused Eric's offer of a drink and they sat quietly for a little while, as the ex-jockey scanned the room, seeking out familiar faces. Finally, satisfied, he turned to Eric. 'Well, the killing of Joe Paulson has raised more than a few pigeons, right enough.'

'How do you mean?'

Parton bared his teeth in a humourless smile. 'There's more than a few people running scared. The big shots were all quick to deny they had any dealings with Joe Paulson, but now he's been done in, they're scared as hell that something damaging is going to crawl out of the woodwork.'

'What have you managed to pick up?' Eric asked.

Jackie Parton ruminated over the question for a while, then shook his head. 'About individuals, not a lot. Other than certain people are running scared. I've heard Lon Stanley's name mentioned but that might be just because he owned Stagshaw, and will be making a big insurance claim. There's some suggestion he might find the cash useful.'

'Because his business is in trouble?'

'Could be. So there's one school of thought, maybe he torched the place himself, or arranged for it to be done. But I think that's mainly guesswork, after the event. On the other hand, I've picked up a rumour about his site manager.'

'Denton.'

'That's the one. He had some deal going, I'm told, handling substances Stagshaw didn't have licences for.'

'What's that got to do with Paulson's death?'

Parton shrugged non-committally. 'Maybe nothing. But you asked me to find out what was being said along the river. As for the gangs . . . there's something odd going on. Maybe it's got to do with Paulson, maybe not. But it involves Mad Jack Tenby.'

'In what way?'

'It's all a bit vague. And, oddly enough, the first bit of gossip came from my enquiries into the *Princess Eugenie.* Like I told you, that sort of stuff is out of my league, really, but I got in touch with my one and only contact at that level of activity, and he didn't really have anything to give me on that piece of business. In fact, he reckoned that the talk was Jason Sullivan would be able to show he was clean enough on the deal. The reckoning is that he'd never been involved with that insurance contract. On the other hand, my contact told me something rather interesting about another bit of financial hokey-pokey. You heard of Holystone Mining?'

Eric recalled Susie Cartwright's comments in the office that afternoon. He nodded. 'Heard of it yes, but no details.'

'Seems the company made a rights issue.

Big things were predicted for the company. Then the shares were sold in the market place soon after. And someone made a right killing. But that's the odd thing. In some way, Jack Tenby was involved.'

'Tenby? Sharedealing doesn't seem quite his scene.'

'That's what's made the riverside buzz a bit. And it has something to do with his girlfriend—Carrie Fane. You come across her?' When Eric shook his head, Parton went on, 'Flash kind of woman. Generation younger than Tenby, but what do you expect? Trophy stuff, really, but seems he's more than a bit hooked on her. Anyway, he's been in a rage and threatening blue murder, because she's lit out south, and it's got something to do with shares in Holystone Mining. There's plenty of rumours flying around . . .' He flicked a quick glance around the bar, paused, and was silent for a little while. 'Don't take a look just yet, but there's a guy at the bar. Came in just after me. Seems somewhat interested in you.'

Eric waited for a few moments then glanced casually around. He groaned. 'Reporter. Name of Preece. He's been to see me this afternoon. He wanted information, to do a story on Paulson. I hope he's not going to be a nuisance.'

Parton shrugged. 'Well, he's not alone in wanting information. It looks as though Tenby is after something over this sharedealing matter. Paulson, it seems, is a lot more popular now he's dead. Everyone wants to get hold of him—or rather, of what he had.' He hesitated. 'And then, there's the other matter.'

'What?'

'Terry Bell: the Batboy.' Jackie Parton's glance slid around the bar, and he seemed to relax a little. Eric looked up also: with relief, he saw that Preece was leaving. He leaned forward as Parton continued. 'When I say that people are wanting to know what Paulson had, the key seems to be that little scallywag Bell.'

'How do you mean, the key?'

'Tenby's looking out for him; and all the chat is Tenby's not alone. I haven't picked up any names other than Mad Jack's, but it looks like a number of people are trying to find Terry Bell—apart from the police.'

Eric was puzzled. He shook his head doubtfully. 'What people? Stanley—Denton? There's the possibility that the boy Ridout saw at Stagshaw might have been Bell, but why should others be looking for him now?'

'It's not Bell they really want. It's Paulson's treasure house.'

Eric stared at the ex-jockey, his thoughts swiftly slipping over what he already knew. 'Joe Paulson showed me a place in Fenham, where he stored documents. Quite a pile. The police have got them now, but Paulson's told me it was relatively unimportant stuff. They'll not find much there. And the farmhouse where Paulson died—it looks like it was fired to get rid of information stored there.'

Parton grunted affirmatively. 'He must have accumulated a hell of a lot of material, but he'd been doing it for years.'

Slowly, Eric said, 'Paulson told me he had three treasure houses—three Pandora boxes. And people are out looking for Terry Bell. But what's the connection?'

Jackie Parton's eyes were serious. 'There was a link between Bell and Paulson. For the last six months or so, Terry's been working as a runner for Paulson. Did some collecting for him, the odd bit of snooping. The Batboy could get in places at night where Paulson couldn't. It was like a Fagin-Artful Dodger arrangement, if you ask me. And the relationship is now out: and people want to talk to Terry Bell.'

'It would be best for him if he went to the police.'

Jackie Parton shook his head. 'No, he won't do that. He doesn't trust them—and if they get their hands on him, there's some offences hanging over him which he thinks will mean a prison sentence for sure. But also, he's running scared. He knows people are looking for him—and since Tenby's one of them he's scared witless. He knows what a baseball bat can do. But . . . I been talking to a friend of his on the Meadow Well estate, and I think I've managed to make him see reason.'

209

'How do you mean?'

'I told this friend that Terry Bell could trust you. That you were straight.' He was silent for a little while, and Eric knew that the ex-jockey's mind was slipping back over events that had occurred six months ago, when he had lost faith in Eric Ward, and felt he had stepped over the line between legality and illegitimacy. He glanced at Eric, and his eyes were careful. 'I gave him my word. If Terry agreed to see you, you'd make sure he was looked after.'

'But . . .' Eric was confused. 'I . . . what does he hope to gain?'

'He knows there are people out there looking for him. He knows what they want. The location of Paulson's last storehouse. And he knows where it is. But if he's caught, and forced to tell them just where Paulson kept his most important documents, what happens then? He could still be in trouble—maybe even deeper. So he'll meet you, talk to you. On my say so. After that, you do what you can to help him, with the police—and remove Tenby and the rest of the lice clinging to his back.'

Jackie Parton's glance swept the room again, uneasily. He glanced at Eric and then nodded, rose to his feet. 'I'll give you a moment to think about it. I'll be back.'

He walked away, vanished towards the back of the lounge bar. Eric sat there for a while, thinking about what Parton had said. A burst of raucous laughter came from the girls

210

nearby: they were rising, getting ready to leave. They passed Jackie Parton as he was coming back to the lounge bar and there were a few shrieks of laughter at what he said to them. Then Jackie rejoined Eric, brushing some drops of water from his collar.

'Starting to rain outside.' He sat down, stared at Eric. Doubts swirled deep in his eyes. 'You made up your mind?'

The last of the Pandora boxes. Eric nodded. 'I'll meet Terry Bell. And I'll do what I can to sort out his problems.'

CHAPTER FIVE

1

Charlie felt a little surge of excitement in his veins. He had the feeling that today might be like a birthday for him, as he stared at the woman he had last seen at the nightclub owned by Mad Jack Tenby.

'Your name? You real name, that is?'

Her mouth was sullen, but resigned. She wriggled uncomfortably in the tight red dress. 'Ludmila.'

'Your surname?'

'My other name is Paderewski.'

'Oh, yes. Like the singer.' His glance slipped to Elaine Start, seated beside him in the interview room. She returned his glance, slightly bored: she knew he was trying to wind her up. He turned back to the Russian girl.

'So, let's have the full story this time. You were picked up at three o'clock, outside the *Moonglow* in Newcastle, and arrested for soliciting. What's going on? Jack Tenby not paying you enough?'

She shrugged. 'He don't treat me like he promised. He's like a mad dog sometimes. He threaten me. I don't like that. I am from Russland.'

Charlie nodded sagely. 'Yes, I'd like to hear

about that. How you got here. From Russland.'

She eyed him carefully for a few moments. 'You got a cigarette?'

He did not smoke himself, but he always kept some for moments like this. He fished in the desk drawer in front of him, took out a half-empty packet, shook out a cigarette and offered it to her. She eyed him coolly, as though he were a customer, and accepted the cigarette and then waited. He glared at her, took out a box of matches, struck one. She accepted the light with a gracious insouciance. Elaine Start coughed lightly, but Charlie ignored her.

Ludmila blew some smoke ceilingwards. 'He didn't treat me right. He promised me things. Nice people. Plenty money. But the men up here, they are not generous men. And the winter—it reminds me of Siberia, you know?'

Charlie grimaced. He knew what she meant. When the February wind came whistling in from the North Sea it could make a man contract like he worked in a harem. 'So he didn't treat you right.'

'He took up with that woman. Carrie, she's called. But she's no better than me. And he forgot his promises to me. Introduce me to nice guys. Make me good money. So I left him. I can do business on my own. So I came in to Newcastle. But it's the same story. Cheapskates.' She eyed him carefully, as though weighing his usefulness to her. 'I want to go to London. There is more money there. And I want some introductions.'

Charlie took a deep breath. She wasn't pulling any punches. But then, she was from Russland. He'd heard that the Russian police were more often than not involved in the rackets themselves. He hesitated, glanced at Elaine Start meaningfully, and nodded. She shook her head in disapproval, but when he frowned at her she murmured something into the recording device, and then switched off the tape. She folded her arms over her splendid breasts, demonstrating her disagreement. He dragged his eyes away from temptation and turned back to Ludmila Paderewski, or whatever her name really was. He didn't care.

'I've got connections in London. Maybe we can drop the soliciting charge. Put you on a train. Introduce you to some people.'

'Is warmer down there, no?'

'It's warmer,' he agreed.

'So what you want to know?' she asked, pushing back her long dyed-blonde hair, red lips parted, one eyebrow arched, eyeing him sensually through a drifting haze of smoke.

'*Bloody Marlene Dietrich*,' he heard Elaine Start mutter under her breath.

*   *   *

Jack Tenby kept them waiting, but Charlie didn't mind. He stood in Tenby's plush, well-

214

appointed office at Wallsend, looking out of the window. In the distance he could see the swing of the river, the funnels of the Bergen Line ferry edging up into the Tyne, bringing Norwegian tourists in for their usual weekend raid on the Newcastle department stores. That was one thing at least about his move north: there was the river. It meant he didn't miss the Thames too much. He reflected that it was strange how rivers seem to attract villainy. He heard the door open behind him.

'Miss Start! We meet yet again. Seen any good films recently?'

'The old ones are the best, Mr Tenby.'

Mad Jack Tenby grinned. He took the comment as a compliment, a veiled hint as to his own attractiveness to young women. Then the smile faded as he turned his head to look at Charlie. 'DCI Spate. First time in my office, I believe.'

'That's right. Nice office. Good location. I was just admiring the view. The estates down there; the docks in the distance; the river rats running down below. You can keep an eye on all the villains you employ, from here.'

'Now, Mr Spate, you know I don't employ villains. I'm a legitimate businessman.'

'Well, as they say, if you can build up a business so it's big enough, it'll look respectable.' Charlie moved away from the widow and took a seat in front of Tenby's spacious, uncluttered desk. There was a box of cigars on the desk. Charlie leaned forward, plucked one out, sniffed it admiringly, and replaced it. Tenby was annoyed at the freedom he took, but after a moment the businessman, with a sharp glance at Elaine Start, moved behind the desk and sat down. 'Trouble is,' Charlie continued easily, 'I've never been convinced you'd left the old habits behind. I'm assured by people in high places that you're legitimate, but I don't believe it. And now . . .'

'Now what?'

'I been talking to a little bird. She's been chirping nicely. Name of Paderewski.'

'Who?'

Charlie chuckled. 'Ludmila. From Russland.'

Jack Tenby's brow darkened. 'That slut.'

'Hey, that's no way to talk of a little girl from Russland who you nurtured, and made promises to, and didn't do right by.'

There was a short silence. At last Tenby growled, 'What's this all about, Mr Spate? I think I know the girl you're talking about, she used to come along to my clubs regular. And I had reason to warn the lads to have a word with her once or twice: I don't mind women coming into the clubs, maybe making deals with the punters—it helps the trade, you know. But they're like the decorations, I see them, but I don't pay attention. Until they become a nuisance.'

'And she became a nuisance?'

216

'She got too obvious. I had to ban her from *Spring Heeled Jacks*,' Tenby said evenly.

'That's not the way she says it happened,' Charlie said flatly.

'That ain't exactly my problem.'

'Oh, but it really is, Mr Tenby. You see, you really pissed off this young lady. Now maybe she doesn't know the way things are run here on the Tyne—you know, do things to the other bugger before he does them to you. Normally, I guess, you wouldn't care if one of your whores made off, particularly if she was making a nuisance of herself. The girls would usually know better than to make a fuss, because they could end up with a scarred face, couldn't they?'

'Mr Spate—'

'But little Ludmila, she's different. She's seen it all before, and maybe harder men than you, back home. She walked out of here on her own bat, and guess what? We picked her up. Working the street outside the *Moonglow*. And she's so niggled, she's been talking.' Charlie smiled thinly. 'And the trouble is, Jack, you can't touch her now. Not while she's under our protection. It's not like the old days, is it? You got too much to lose, putting the arm on her.'

'Just what has the little tart been saying?' Jack Tenby snarled.

'Life story,' Charlie replied happily. 'And you know, it's really interesting, hearing someone's life story, though it can be bloody if

217

you got to live it, I guess. We started at the beginning. Vladivostok, of all places. Her father was a merchant seaman. With incestuous leanings. So she left home at fourteen. Soon found friends to look after her —at a price. She moved around. She doesn't like the cold. It was cold in Finland, when she ended up there. So she moved further south. Drifted to the bright lights and warmer evenings. Until one day she got picked up by your business connections in Amsterdam. And shipped across the Channel. Zeebrugge to Hull, on the ferry. She enjoyed that, she says. And she quite liked what you had to say to her. Not exactly breathing promises of undying love, but money, flash cars, a comfortable life nestling up to a bad old man. But with Ludmila, money is like snow in her hands—it sort of just melts away. And when she saw someone else in the picture, and she was having to work for her money again—putting out in the clubs, she got sort of resentful.'

'Just what are you getting at, Mr Spate?' Tenby's tone was controlled, but his eyes were flickering uneasily. 'You don't believe the crap this tart's been feeding you, surely!'

'Believe it? Why should the poor girl lie?' Charlie asked ironically. 'But I'll tell you what I'm getting at. You've tried to show the posh friends you've bought that you're nothing more than an old, reformed rogue. That your muscle days are behind you. That all that is

218

something to laugh about over a malt whisky or a bottle of champagne in the club, now that you're a legitimate businessman. But I've never been convinced. When the Tyneside mob got shaken up a year ago, you decided to come back in—or maybe you'd never walked away. But I'm bloody certain that you're backing the drugs scene on the Tyne—'

'You can't prove that!' Tenby snapped, reddening angrily.

'That's right, I can't,' Charlie agreed mildly. 'We pulled in Danny Blanchard a few weeks back, but he's not talking, and we can't yet show a link to you. But you know, all castles, they crumble in time. You pull out a stone or two, here and there, and the castle crumbles even faster. That's where Ludmila comes in.'

'What are you getting at?'

'You're projecting the image of a successful businessman, but the image is built on something else.'

'*The Great Gatsby*,' Elaine Start murmured. 'You'll remember the film, Mr Tenby.'

'Alan Ladd,' he said sourly. 'It was crap.'

Irritated at the intervention, Charlie went on, 'It's true that it's unlikely I'll be able to prove your involvement in the drugs run on the river. But your castle isn't secure. Ludmila's given us the opportunity to pull a couple of keystones out of the wall. She's a whore—we all know that. It's the story of her life. And she admits it. But she tells me she was brought here by you and your organisation. She tells me she's not alone. There's a big business in the north—Newcastle, Sunderland, Teesside, Middlesbrough, York—all the northern cities are getting a regular supply of girls from Eastern Europe. Quite a lucrative business for the ringmasters. And you're one of them. With Ludmila, we can crack open the ring. Oh, it's not such a good haul for us as pinning drugdealing on you, but it'll give us a start. Bringing in girls for immoral purposes. Living off the earnings of prostitution.'

'You can't make it stick.' Tenby's voice was rising in anger. 'Who's going to believe that tart—'

'I believe her,' Charlie replied.

'It'll get thrown out. No one's going to take it seriously.'

'Ha, but there's the rub,' Charlie insisted. 'Some people will take it seriously. Of course, at the moment, they can smile and shrug off stories about what you did as a young man, The lovable rogue, is that how they see you? But your friends in the county set, with their big houses in Northumberland, and their dinner parties . . . they been giving you the respectability, and the contacts you like, Jack. Isn't that so? The lad from the back streets, made it good, living high and hob-nobbing with the upper crust. But what's going to happen when we haul you in on a charge of running whores in from Europe? You think

220

they're going to stick with you then, Jack? Not bloody likely. You'll see, there's more than a few doors going to close on you, believe me.'

'This can't be happening,' Mad Jack Tenby muttered thickly.

'It's happening,' Charlie assured him. 'First bit of stone out of the wall. Truth is, Jack, women will have been your downfall. You should never have picked up with Carrie Fane. Ludmila got edged out, and she didn't like it. Now if you'd treated her right, and not persuaded Carrie into your bed—'

'Stupid cow!' Tenby suddenly burst out.

'Ludmila?' Charlie shrugged. 'I guess she is, really. She's taking a chance, and she'll find that life in London can be just as cold as it is here up north. But it's what she wants. And it's a deal we'll cut with her.'

'I wasn't talking about that Russian bitch!' Tenby rose, placed his battered knuckles on the desk and leaned forward menacingly. 'I was talking about Carrie Fane.'

Charlie stared up at the angry man towering above him. 'What's the matter? She skipped out on you as well?'

'Look here, Spate, I've never been one to be browbeaten,' Tenby growled. 'And this Russian thing, I don't think you'll be able to make it stick. It'd be her word—and she's just a whore. My brief would tear her to shreds if it got to court. But . . . I got to admit, her shouting the odds in public could make life a little . . .

uneasy for me, for a while. You wouldn't make the charges stick, but with that sort of mud flying around . . .'

'So what's your point, Tenby?' Charlie asked curiously.

'The Ludmila thing is peanuts. But I'll do you a trade.'

Suspicion stained Charlie Spate's voice. 'What sort of trade?'

'You back off on the Ludmila thing, leave me alone, and I'll give you something bigger.'

'Like what?' Charlie scoffed, making no effort to disguise his contempt.

Mad Jack Tenby's eyes were glittering. 'I'll tell you all about Carrie Fane.'

2

Jackie Parton had insisted that he and Eric set off in separate cars, hinting darkly that he had business of his own to attend to. Eric was disinclined to argue: he had no real idea about how the ex-jockey made a living, and he had no doubt Jackie had many irons in the fire. Some of them, he probably would not want Eric to know about. So when Jackie called at the flat in Gosforth in the late afternoon, Eric got into the Celica, and agreed to follow him. The only clue Parton gave to their destination was that it was north of Newcastle.

They drove out of the city on the A1, heading for Morpeth. Jackie Parton's car was a somewhat battered Vauxhall and he drove in a curiously sedate manner, so Eric had no problem keeping in visual touch with him as they ran along the dual carriageway. Just short of Morpeth Jackie turned off to follow the coast road. Eric knew it well enough: he and Anne had often taken the road to Craster to walk along the coast route, over the greensward past the dramatic ruins of Dunstanburgh Castle, and along the empty, windswept sands that gave a long vista towards the castled headland of Bamburgh. Now, as he followed Jackie Parton's Vauxhall along the narrow winding road, catching occasional glimpses of the darkening sea, Eric thought again about those walks. He wondered whether there would ever be a return to those experiences, with Anne. Somehow, depressingly, he doubted it.

When Jackie Parton turned to avoid entering the decaying fishing port of Amble, Eric realised they would not be going as far as the long coastline at Craster. The road ran along the river Aln, and ahead of them he could see the ancient pile of Warkworth; they drove past the mediaeval fortified gate bridge and swung down towards the looping roads that took them to the harbour on the other side of the river mouth. Fine shimmering sands stretched into the distance at the old fishing village, where the Aln met the North Sea. Beyond the broad beach lay the familiar jumble of houses and old inns on the hill overlooking the old harbour. Some of the houses in the town had been converted from eighteenth century granaries, because for centuries Alnmouth had been a great shipbuilding and grain port until a violent storm had changed the course of the river in 1806, rendering it useless for shipping. Now, with its beach, and golf course, and brightly painted leisure craft moored in the estuary it was nothing more than a quiet tourist backwater, sheltering under the grassy hill crowned by the church dedicated to St Waleric, also destroyed in the great storm of the early nineteenth century.

Jackie Parton pulled in to the kerb on the quiet, gently sloping road, flanked with Victorian villas and stopped. Eric parked the Celica just behind him. Jackie got out and looked around. He gestured towards a stolid, bay-fronted house with a small front garden. Eric looked at the house, and was aware of a slight movement behind the curtains on the ground floor. 'Is this it?'

'What Paulson called Pandora Three,' Parton said, flickering quick glances around the harbour. 'The boy's inside. He'll be expecting you.'

'Aren't you coming in?' Eric asked doubtfully. 'It would be better if you did—he might get anxious if I go in alone.'

Parton squinted at the darkening sky and

shook his head. 'I got other things to do. And Terry Bell's seen me with you. He's already clocked us from the window. He won't be doing a runner. You go on in. But first, take the car around the back. There's no parking allowed just here, but you should be able to use the lane behind the house.'

Reluctantly, Eric nodded, drove the car to the end of the road, and swung into the lane behind. He locked the car, then walked around to the front of the house again. As he opened the gate, and walked up the short drive to the house, Jackie Parton waved briefly to him and drove away, heading back up past the line of hotels and cafes that made up the main street of Alnmouth. From the front entrance of the house Eric watched him go, then turned and tapped on the door.

*   *   *

Jackie Parton drove out towards the loop road, and up to the grassy hill. He parked his battered vehicle just behind the church, picked up a pair of binoculars from the back seat, locked the car and walked down the hill, taking a back road to the beach. Below him the river meandered through its sandy estuary, dull under the darkening sky: the tide was out, sandy banks exposed, pleasure craft leaning at angles, beached on the muddy river edges. Jackie made his way along the twisting path

225

through the hummocks overlooking the golf course. The wind had lifted as the sky darkened, and the breakers were rising, crashing noisily on the beach. There was a scattering of cars parked on the front, facing the wild sea spray. He ignored them, selected a deserted spot among the sandy dunes and knelt down. He smoothed out a small area, removing some rough stones and then he lay down on his side. He removed the binoculars from their leather case, turned onto his stomach, and focussed the glasses. The church on the hill sprang into his vision: he moved his line of sight down, until he could pick out the front of the house where he had left Eric Ward, checked his view of the back lane. He adjusted the focussing screw. Then he waited.

*　　　*　　　*

When Eric tapped on the door there was a pause. He heard a light shuffling from the corridor, and after a moment the door was eased open. Eric pushed it lightly with his hand and stepped into the gloom of the passageway beyond. The boy stood at the foot of the stairs, tense, as though poised, ready for flight.

'Terry?' Eric's voice echoed in the passageway, as though the house was empty. 'I'm Eric Ward.'

The boy stared at him. He was small, thin,

undersized, with a badly nourished look about him. He wore jeans and trainers, a dark leather windcheater, and his face was lean and pale, his hollowed eyes uneasy, with a hunted look in their depths. His reddish hair was untidy, uncombed. He looked scared and uncertain, and Eric guessed it would not take much to make him run.

'Jackie Parton—that was him outside.' Eric said quietly. 'He set up this meeting.'

'Where's he gone now?' the boy asked suspiciously.

Eric shrugged. 'He said he had business of his own to attend to.'

'He's gone for the polis,' Terry Bell accused, his voice shaky and uncertain.

'No. He gave your friend a promise and he'll keep it. So will I.'

There was a long silence. Terry Bell stood there, one hand on the balustrade at the foot of the stairs, poised, still ready to run, alert. 'They reckon you're straight,' the boy said at last, grudgingly, still uncertain. 'And you'll be able to help me.'

Eric hesitated, then nodded. 'I'll do what I can. If you help me.' He glanced around him. 'Does . . . did this house belong to Joe Paulson?'

There was a short silence, then Terry Bell nodded. 'He met me here a few times.'

'You worked for him?'

'On and off. Just the last few months.' Terry

227

Bell hesitated, his mouth twisting with doubt. 'They're looking for me, the polis, and the rest of them. But I don't know anything, believe me.'

'You knew where this place was, 'Eric said slowly. 'Maybe that's enough.'

Terry Bell hesitated, then nodded. He stood awkwardly, thinking, staring at Eric as though he was still not sure and then abruptly he turned, gestured to Eric to follow him, and he led the way up the uncarpeted stairs. Their steps echoed eerily: the house was unfurnished, Eric realised. It had never been used by Joe Paulson to live in. It was merely a storehouse, a treasure house, a Pandora box for the night walker.

Terry Bell led the way to the room at the end of the short corridor. He stepped inside. Eric followed. He was surprised. He had seen the mass of paper at Paulson's house in Fenham—it had been piled high, scattered about. Here, things had been managed differently. The room was bare, uncarpeted, and contained no furniture other than two filing cabinets. As the boy watched, Eric walked forward and opened the top drawer of the first cabinet. Inside, documents were filed neatly, in a carefully labelled suspended filing system. Eric guessed that it was here Paulson had retained the documents he regarded as important: he would have sifted these from the mass that he had kept stored in Fenham, and

228

at the farmhouse. He had been a careful man. He had known how dangerous some of the documents could be—to other people, but also to him.

Eric glanced curiously at Terry Bell. 'What exactly did you do for Paulson?'

The boy shrugged. He had looked small, vulnerable downstairs in the corridor, but now suddenly there was a certain air of cocky pride in his manner. 'He wasn't quick, like me,' he explained. 'There were places he couldn't go. And he'd heard about me. I got my name in the papers. Regular. But he didn't care that I was in bother. He got in contact: he made a deal with me. Now and again he'd get hold of me at Meadow Well, say he wanted me to do a job for him. Couple of times it meant breaking and entering, you know. Couple of times, I had to go over the roof, but that was a piece of cake for me. You seen what they wrote about me?'

Eric ignored the swagger in the boy's tone. 'What was it he wanted from you on these occasions?'

'Varied. Usually, documents, papers. I dunno what it was all about really. But I gathered that he went through all the stuff he got out of the skips and suchlike, and then maybe he got a lead of some sort. That's when he'd ask me to go in, ferret around. If possible, I had to do it neat, like no one had been in. So they wouldn't know. If I couldn't do that, I was to take something, make it look like a regular burglary. I could keep anything I took. He didn't want it. He wasn't a fence, or nothin' like that.' He paused, thinking. 'I dunno really what he wanted the stuff for. He never told me.'

Obsession, Eric thought. Paulson had started seeking out secrets, and in the end had gained so many he didn't really know what to do with them. But he'd always known they were dangerous, and in the end one had been too dangerous. It had led to his death.

'You'd been to his place at Fenham?' When the boy nodded, Eric asked, 'And the farmhouse, near Stagshaw?'

The reply was slow coming. Terry Bell cast a glance around the room, as though making sure there was an escape route available. Then he nodded.

'Were you there when Paulson was killed?'

The silence that followed his question hung around them coldly, like a shroud. Terry Bell was staring at him, uncertainty registered in every line of his small body. He had always run from trouble: he seemed ready to run again. At last he muttered, 'I had nothin' to do with what went on there, Mr Ward. I didn't even know what it was all about. They said Jackie Parton told them you'd help me. But you got to make the polis believe, it was nothin' to do with me.'

'What happened at Stagshaw, Terry?'

230

The boy shuffled, looked about him as though wishing he could be anywhere but here. 'You got to realise, Mr Ward, I didn't know what was going on. I was just doing the odd job for Mr Paulson. And he paid me well enough. And there was the stuff I picked up on the side. But I had to be careful, becos the polis were lookin' for me, you know?'

There was a short, uneasy silence. 'Go on,' Eric persuaded gently.

Terry Bell shrugged his narrow shoulders. 'The last few days I saw him, Mr Paulson, he was different from before. He was mad about something. Angry I think it was about having to go to court. I told him it was no big deal appearin' in court, I'd been up plenty times, he got really niggled when I said that. He said there was bastards out there who had used him, but were now denyin' him, like he was some kind of Judas. He said they wasn't going to get away with it: he had things on them that he hadn't used, but they'd find out he wasn't going to go down quietly.'

'Did he mention names?'

'I guess so.' Terry Bell twisted his scrawny neck around, as though listening for echoes of the past. 'But I didn't pay no attention, really, when he started shoutin' the odds. But I do know he was really mad. And there was a couple of things he asked me to do. Couple of jobs. But one of them was different.'

'How do you mean?'

231

Terry Bell shuffled uneasily. 'It wasn't the usual thing, looking for papers and that stuff. He gave me a camera. Asked me to go up on a roof. Get a shot.'

'Of what?'

'Uh, you know. This bloke and this girl.'

Eric was puzzled. 'A couple? Why?'

The boy giggled, nervously. 'They was screwin', like.'

An uneasy silence grew around them. Eric stared at him, not quite understanding. 'You mean he wanted you to get a pornographic photograph?'

'Naw, he didn't do that sort of stuff, I don't think. I mean, he had some stuff on pervs who liked kids, but he wasn't no collector himself. He just asked me to get up there, and when this bird went in, to get a shot of them together. I don't know what he wanted it for. Anyway, I got it, but I nearly got caught. I had to go over the roofs like I was flyin', I tell you. Then, few days later, Mr Paulson called me to meet him at the farmhouse, to pay me.'

'What happened then?'

Terry Bell wandered around the room, rubbing his thin arm in a nervous gesture. 'I didn't know what the hell was going on, I swear it, Mr Ward. You got to tell that to the polis. It was nuthin' to do with me. I'd only got to the farmhouse late afternoon, had no car, had to take a bus, like, and walk up to the site. I thought I could have twocked a car for meself at Meadow Well, but there was no joy. Me, on a bus!' He grunted in annoyance at the thought. 'But I'd only been at the farmhouse a few minutes when this car drives up, parks besides Mr Paulson's car. Mr Paulson, he looked kind of pleased, sort of satisfied, you know, but he told me to make myself scarce. So I went upstairs, and I heard this guy come in and they was talking, and after a while when they started coming up the stairs I did the usual: up into the loft space. And then things turned nasty.'

'How do you mean?'

'I wasn't paying too much attention, tell you the truth, but there was a bit of shouting going on. This guy was threatening Mr Paulson, he wanted something from him and then suddenly I heard a bang, a sort of thudding, and Mr Paulson was groaning. After that, it went quiet for a bit and then I could hear someone walking around the room, turning things over. Then this guy was swearing, rampaging through the room, paper being thrown everywhere. In a little while, he went downstairs and things got quiet again.'

'Could you see who it was?' Eric asked.

Terry Bell shook his head. 'There was no way. I was in the loft—the hatch closed. But when everythin' went silent, I moved the hatch, looked out. I didn't like what I saw, not one little bit. There he was. Mr Paulson was lyin' on the floor. He wasn't moving and the papers by his head was all sort of wet and dark stained. When I looked closer I could see his head was all sort of bashed in. That's when I knew I was really in trouble.'

'What did you do?'

The boy cleared his throat nervously. 'I was scared as hell. I pulled back the hatch, dropped into the room. I can do that sort of thing real quiet, you know? I came to the top of the stairs and was just about to go down when I saw this guy in the hallway. He had his back to me. He was piling up paper and documents, all sort of rubbish. And he must have been out to his car, I guess 'cos he'd got a petrol can from was sloshing the stuff around. I knew then exactly what he was going to do, and I knew this was no place for Terry Bell to hang around. So I went back to the bedroom, sneaked out through the window, dropped onto the sloping roof above the kitchen at the back and came around the side of the house. I thought of just leggin' it at first, but I was afraid he might see me crossing the space to the hill, and maybe give chase, and I didn't want my head bashed in like Mr Paulson. So instead I ducked down into Mr Paulson's car.'

It was what Eddie Ridout had seen from the hill—the boy, sneaking out of the house, entering the car, crouching down.

'I been used to twockin,' Terry Bell was saying with a hint of nervous pride. 'Some reckon I'm one of the best. It was no great

234

problem. I hotwired her quick, and drove out of there like a bat out of hell. He'd have seen me go, but there wasn't nuthin' he could do about it. And I guessed he didn't know who I was.' He paused, ruminating. 'I left the car at a piece of waste ground in Scotswood. I knew it wouldn't be left standing there long. Sure enough, day or so later, some of the kids used it, raced it around a while, then torched it.'

'You didn't have a good look at the man who killed Joe Paulson?' Eric asked slowly.

Terry Bell shook his head. 'Naw, not really. And I didn't want to know. You got to understand all this was too much for me, Mr Ward, out of my league.'

'Why didn't you go to the police?'

'You crazy? What do you think they'd do to me? I got no reason to deal with the blue, no, sir. I wanted to stay well out of this: it was too heavy for the likes of me. Besides, they're after me for robbery.'

'So what did you do?'

'I laid low, like it was the sensible thing to do. But then the talk on the river made me nervous. It had got out that I'd been doing some stuff for Mr Paulson, and after he got killed, I heard there was questions being asked. I knew the polis were after me, and that's one thing, it's natural, I can handle that, but when I get to hear there's villains after talking to me as well, that's when I get to feel I need protection.' He shivered suddenly. 'You

235

got to help me, Mr Ward.'

Eric considered what he had been told. 'It's a pity you didn't get a look at the killer.'

'Ha, well, I didn't get a good look at him, couldn't tell you who he was,' Bell replied reluctantly. 'But I think from what I did see, and some of the things I heard when they was arguin', that it was the guy in the photograph.'

'Photograph?'

'The one I took on the roof. Through the skylight window.' Eric frowned. An edge of excitement tugged at his chest. 'Do you know where Joe Paulson kept that photograph?'

Terry Bell hesitated. 'That guy—the one who killed Mr Paulson—he was looking for it at the farmhouse. That's what he was there for. But Mr Paulson never kept his best stuff anywhere but here. And I seen where he put it.' He turned, walked across to the second filing cabinet. He opened the lower drawer, and extracted a brown paper envelope. He handed it to Eric.

'I guess I wasn't cut out to be a photographer,' he muttered mournfully.

Eric took the envelope from him and opened it. Inside was a glossy print, some eight inches by six. It was of a woman, naked, blonde hair over her face. She was lying on her back, startled. Standing at the side of the bed, staring up towards the skylight, was a man, unclothed, hand raised, half shielding his face. But the whole thing was fuzzy, unfocussed.

236

As Terry Bell had admitted, he wasn't cut out to be a photographer.

Eric stared at the photograph. There was something familiar about the man, even though Eric could make out only half of the hazy features. He had a sudden, unwelcome vision in his mind, of Anne, naked, with Jason Sullivan. He thrust the thought aside angrily, then slid the photograph back into the envelope. 'Come on. We'd better get out of here.'

'Where we going?' Terry Bell asked fearfully.

'Back to Newcastle,' Eric replied.

'You promised you'd look after me on this, Mr Ward.' Terry Bell wailed, as he followed Eric down the stairs, his trainers scuffing lightly on the boards.

'I'll keep my promise, Terry—but we've got to go now for the police.'

3

The boy was reluctant. Eric took him by the arm, and pulled him along out into the back yard of the house. He walked down the narrow pathway to the battered wooden door in the tall stone wall. Beyond the wall was the back lane where he had parked the Celica.

He pushed open the door, walked to the car, half dragging the protesting boy. Still holding Terry Bell's arm with his left hand, he fished for his car keys, envelope tucked under his arm. As he did so, there was a sudden jerk, a thud, and Terry Bell was a dead weight, falling to the ground. Eric half turned, saw the boy on the ground beside the car, and then stared at the man standing there with the gun in his hand.

'Unlock the car, and shove him in the back.'

Under the menace of the gun, Eric did as he was told.

Behind the wheel, Eric was aware of the light snoring sound emerging from Terry Bell's mouth. He glanced back. The boy was slumped in the seat, a thin trickle of blood oozing from behind his ear. The man in the passenger seat beside him grunted, pushed the muzzle of the pistol in his ribs. 'Let's make one thing clear, in case you get any stupid ideas. I spent five years in the Army. I know how to use this thing. Now, the envelope.'

Eric leaned forward, picked it from the floor where he had dropped it.

'Open it.'

Eric did as he was told. He slipped the photograph out, held it up for the gunman to inspect it.

'Jesus!' the man gritted angrily.

'That's right,' Eric said quietly. 'It's fuzzy. The boy was no photographer. It's unlikely you could ever have been identified from that photograph.'

'Shut up!'

He sat glaring at the photograph, the gun pushing hard against Eric's ribcage. His mouth was working in frustration.

'It was a bad mistake, killing Paulson—'

'I said *shut up!*' Suddenly, the gunman seemed to have come to a decision. He crumpled the photograph, pushing it into his pocket. 'All right, drive. Let's get away from here. And remember—' The gun muzzle was prodded fiercely at Eric's ribs. 'I know how to use this thing.'

Eric started the car, and they moved out of the lane. Under the passenger's directions he headed away from the town on the back road, returning towards the coast road but turning north, towards Craster. Eric's mind was racing. It was late afternoon, the sky was darkening and storm clouds lay out to sea. He thought wildly about how he could turn the tables on the man at his side. He could try to attract attention, but that would be useless. He drove slowly, waiting, thinking, wondering what the gunman had in mind. He could guess: both the boy and he would be ending up like Joe Paulson. And at the moment there was nothing he could do to prevent it.

They bypassed Boulmer, swung out to the loneliness of the headlands beyond. They drove silently, the grey sea rolling in thunderously to their right, the only sound in the car being the stertorous snoring of the unconscious boy on the back seat. Then, as the

Celica breasted the rise and they came to the top of the hill, the man with the gun told him to slow down. 'That parking area up ahead. Stop there.'

Eric pulled in on the black dirt of the makeshift layby. It was a tourist spot: from here visitors could look out to sea, down at the dark craggy rocks of the shore line, a hundred feet below, and in good weather they would make out the distant line of the Farne Islands out to sea, and northwards, the massive fortress on the headland at Bamburgh. 'What exactly did Paulson have on you?' Eric asked.

The man stared at him for a moment, distracted. 'What did he have on me? The bloody connection. Now leave it. I want to think.'

'What connection?'

The man was irritated, his mouth working uncertainly. He glared at Eric, then said, 'Get the boy out of the back.'

As Eric got out of the car, the gunman slid out also, keeping the gun levelled at him. Fifteen yards away, the waves thundered on the base of the cliff. Eric pushed the front seat forward, reaching for Terry Bell. The body was inert, but he was still breathing. Eric lifted him out with difficulty, laid him down on the sward. Far out to sea the grey-black sky was rent by a flicker of lightning, and a few moments later he heard the rumble of thunder. 'What now?' he asked, standing up.

The man seemed uncertain, still thinking. The gun in his hand was steady, and Eric knew he was willing to use it. 'What connection?' Eric asked, if only to distract him.

'Connection? With a hundred and fifty thousand, that's what!' But he had made up his mind. Eric saw it in his eyes.

The man started to walk forward, skirting alongside the Celica and that moment Eric heard the sound of a car engine in the road below, coming up from Alnmouth. The gunman paused; a few moments later a battered old Vauxhall came slowly around the bend. The man with the gun leaned against the side of the Celica, half hiding the weapon, but still keeping the muzzle pointing in Eric's direction. Eric realised this was the only chance he was going to get. He tensed, ready to throw himself sideways, and then before he could move the sound of the Vauxhall engine suddenly changed, increasing in volume, rising to a protesting roar. The car straightened out of the bend and came hurtling towards them. The gunman stood there, paralysed for a moment as the big vehicle charged towards him and then he flung himself sideways, scrabbling at the bonnet of the Celica to save himself.

The Vauxhall cannoned into Eric's car and he heard the scream of tortured, grinding metal. The Celica bounced, shuddered, was lifted bodily to crash sideways into the gorse

241

bushes at the edge of the layby, while the driver's door of the Vauxhall was torn off. The old car came to a shuddering halt, swivelling into the layby, and freed from his shock, Eric at last came to his senses. He rushed around to the side of the battered Celica.

The gun was lying in the road. Its owner had been thrown sideways under the impact; a glancing blow from the Vauxhall had thrown him towards the gorse bushes. There was blood among the yellow flowers; the man's head was badly torn and scratched by the sharp thorns of the bushes. He was unconscious, but he was still alive.

The engine of the Vauxhall was cut. There was a sudden silence, then the driver's door was kicked away by a vicious foot. Jackie Parton got out, disgustedly. 'This is going to cost you the price of two cars,' he said accusingly. 'Mine's not worth repairing—and yours will be a write-off, if you ask me.'

He peered at the man who lay sprawled, half-hidden in the bushes. 'Is it who I guessed it might be?'

It had started to rain, a cold light spattering of drops, streaking on the bloodied face of the unconscious man.

'Karl Preece,' Eric replied, bending over Terry Bell, as the boy stirred, muttering incoherently. 'Not that you'd have been able to make him out from the photograph he was so keen to get hold of.'

'I don't approve of it, Mr Ward,' Susie Cartwright pronounced as she stood in his office, glaring at him, wincing as he settled himself in his chair. 'If you encouraged the right kind of clients in your practice, you wouldn't get involved in this sort of nonsense. You could have got yourself killed.'

'I would have been, if Jackie Parton hadn't turned up.'

'And that's another one you shouldn't be involved with,' she said in prim disapproval. 'What was he doing there, anyway?' she added, unable to restrain her curiosity.

Jackie had explained it to Eric later, after they'd called the police.

'In my business, you always got to be prepared. That day in the Northumberland Fusilier, when Karl Preece came in, and you told me he'd already been in to see you, something knotted me stomach. There'd been various rumours along the river, some odd feelers being put out, and I'd heard that some journalist had been to see an old friend of mine. Buying some electronic gear. So when I saw Preece there, and you told me who he was, I had a gut feeling. Like I said, you got to be prepared. I was curious. You remember I left you in the pub? Well, I went outside, and I saw him walking away from the car park. So I took

243

a look at your car. I always keep this little device. It's a detector. I checked your car out. Someone had placed a homing device under your Celica. Someone was hoping you'd help them trace Terry Bell. It was my guess maybe it was this guy, walking away from the car park.'

'That's why you wanted us to go to Anmouth in separate cars?' Eric had asked.

'That's right. So I could have freedom of action. I'd taken it easy on the North Road, so he wouldn't find it too difficult, following the homing device. I couldn't be certain it was Preece, but I'd wondered. I settled down among the dunes with my binoculars. I saw the car drive down, wander around a bit. Saw Preece get out, but I still couldn't quite make out who it was. But he headed for the back lane. I moved my vantage point but there wasn't much I could do when I saw you drive out with him in the passenger seat of the Celica. So I legged it back to the car, and followed you.'

'I owe you, Jackie.'

'Haven't you always?'

*   *   *

It was too long, and too complicated to explain to Susie. She hesitated, a little annoyed with him but sympathetic too. She eyed him uncertainly. 'There's someone in the outer

244

office, who wants to see you. But I'm not sure
. . . if you don't feel up to it . . .'

'Who is it?'

'Mr Sullivan.'

He hesitated, a cold feeling in the pit of his
stomach. Then he nodded, reluctantly. 'Ask
him to come in.'

Jason Sullivan entered a few moments later.
He stood in front of Eric's desk. 'You look like
hell. Perhaps this is a bad time.'

'I'm all right. What is it you want to see me
about?'

Jason Sullivan's nostrils twitched; his eyes
were cold, his tone cool but determined. 'I've
had a discussion with Anne. She asked me
certain questions. They annoyed me. I asked
where she'd got these scurrilous rumours from.
It seems they emanated from you.'

'If you're talking about the queries
surrounding the insurance contracts on the
Princess Eugenie, that's right. I warned her
there might be a problem.'

'We're talking libel here, Ward.'

'Not if the rumours are true.'

'They are not.' Jason Sullivan stared at Eric;
his glance was supercilious. 'I've already
explained myself to the Benchers at my Inn.
They've accepted my explanation. I was with
Equitable and Marine. But I took nothing, no
influence with me, when I joined Martin and
Channing. And whatever they find when they
finally dredge the *Princess Eugenie* up from the

245

bottom, it'll in no way inculpate me. Any other suppositions will merely be media nonsense—fishing in murky waters. I've done nothing to be ashamed of. And nothing illegal.' He paused, his lips curling unpleasantly. 'But all this isn't really about insurance contracts, is it? We both know better: it's about Anne.'

Eric was suddenly tired and irritated beyond measure. He got to his feet, somewhat shakily. 'Sullivan, I think Anne made a mistake putting you on the board of Martin and Channing. I think there are still questions to be answered with regard to the part you played in an insurance fraud whatever your Benchers think about it—but then again, I suspect in the long run neither company involved will want too much dirty washing to be aired. So maybe nothing will come of it, even after they do raise the *Princess Eugenie*. As for the rest—I don't like you. I don't know what the hell is going on between you and Anne—if anything—and I don't want to know. Now I've got other, more urgent things to do. So get the hell out of my office!'

Jason Sullivan held his ground for a long moment, then he grunted in contempt, turned, and left. After he had gone, Susie Cartwright looked in at the open door, and then closed it quietly without comment.

And Eric had lied. He didn't have other things to do. Nothing urgent, anyway. Eddie Ridout had asked him to arrange the sale of his farm. He was moving further north—to do what, he was uncertain, but at least he'd have his share of the compensation Lon Stanley was now committed to pay. And the Stagshaw site was to be closed. The explosion, and, it seemed, certain licence irregularities meant that Lon Stanley's operations in the north were over. Eric would be representing the Ewart villagers. But none of these matters was urgent.

And Terry Bell: the head wound had not been serious, and he would be up in court but not for a few days. Eric laid his head back on his chair and closed his eyes. In a little while, the pain would come again, he had no doubt, the feral scratching at his eyeballs. He wondered where his life was going.

He thought about Paulson, the nightwalker, and his treasure houses, and he thought about the legend of Pandora's box. It had contained all the evils and miseries of the world. Pandora's curiosity had made her open it and she had released them all, to plague the world. But what had been the last one to emerge? Ah, yes.

Hope. So there was always that, he considered: hope.

The Chief Constable inspected the file on the desk in front of him with an air of accusation and disgust, as though he found dealing with the minutiae of criminal activity a task that degraded him. He glared at Charlie Spate. 'All right, so what've you got?'

Charlie cleared his throat. 'The civil servant from the Department of the Environment— Palmer-Penrose. He's finally given us the information we wanted.'

'About the Gateshead laboratory?'

Charlie nodded. 'That's right. He's finally admitted their paperwork was defective, and there was a fiddle going on. The Stagshaw site manager, James Denton, he had a deal going. One of the Gateshead people was bypassing the Exeter incineration system, sifting out cash set aside for the contract. Denton was taking the BSE-contaminated drums, money was being exchanged, the Gateshead staff pocketed their share, and it was a nice little racket. Denton's been interviewed. He'll be charged in the morning, along with a couple of people from Gateshead.'

'And the owner of the Stagshaw site?'

Charlie Spate shrugged. 'Denton reckons it was all his idea, and Lon Stanley didn't know about it. So Stanley is in the clear. Not that he's very happy, of course, because the mere fact the BSE-contaminated waste was on site undercuts his defence against the Ewart Village people and makes things worse for him. He'll have to pay compensation—and it looks to me like the whole site will have to close down. So Palmer-Penrose reckons, anyway. Vindictive streak in that man. He's got egg on his face over the BSE stuff, and he'll take it out on Stanley by way of refusal of further licences, and withdrawal of the existing ones.'

The Chief Constable leaned back in his chair, hooded eyes observing Charlie. 'Which brings us to Karl Preece.'

Charlie Spate gritted his teeth. He could guess what was coming.

The Chief Constable's tone was sneering as he tapped the file in front of him with a disbelieving finger. 'So you're saying here you *would* have laid your hands on Preece for the killing of Paulson in time, *eventually*. Except that this solicitor Ward got there first.'

Charlie knew that the Chief Constable was baiting him. Doggedly, he said, 'It would only have been a matter of time, sir. But I'd only just managed to get the information about Carrie Fane. We'd have cracked her quickly enough, once we'd got hold of her, and that would have taken us to Preece. But yes, as it happened, Preece was trying to get hold of the Batboy to silence him, and get hold of any evidence Paulson had had on the connection between Preece and Fane, and, well, the tables got turned on him.'

He didn't want to go into the details with the Chief Constable: he wasn't even sure of them himself, since Eric Ward was somewhat reticent in describing the part played by Jackie Parton. The ex-jockey was reluctant to get too closely involved in police enquiries.

'So fill me in on this *connection*,' the Chief Constable ordered wearily.

'As far as we've got, it seems that Carrie Fane—Mad Jack Tenby's girlfriend—had started an affair with the journalist Karl Preece. And he cooked up a scheme. He runs a financial column—share-tipping. The idea was he'd boost the share issue of Holystone Mining, the way he'd already done with Sandhurst Securities in his national weekend column by giving it an extremely favourable write-up, implying a takeover bid, while she bought in on his behalf on the Friday previous. By the following week the rumours he'd planted meant the share prices had rocketed, she sold out again, and they pocketed something like a hundred and fifty thousand. With no money up front. It was a sucker deal especially when the prices collapsed shortly afterwards.'

'The Stock Exchange would have started an investigation,' the Chief Constable frowned.

'They always do, in such circumstances. And the trail would have led to Carrie Fane. But while there was no connection to be shown between the tipster, Karl Preece, and the beneficiary—Carrie Fane—they would have been able to pin nothing on the journalist tipster. The trouble facing Karl Preece—who'd be facing a jail sentence if it all came out, was that Joe Paulson, in his sniffing around, had picked up on the fact that Jack Tenby's girlfriend was having it away with Preece. So he sent young Terry Bell—the Batboy—around to get a shot of them together. It seems the kid muffed it. He's good at roofs, but not with cameras. But Preece didn't know that. He'd already had threats from Paulson when he refused to support him in the charges brought against the nightwalker, and he guessed it would be Paulson who'd got the photograph so he went after him. Beat him to death at the farmhouse—but he didn't know Terry Bell was in the farmhouse, until the boy scarpered with Paulson's car. So Karl Preece was hunting for him.'

'And this solicitor, Eric Ward?'

'Paulson had been his client. Preece guessed maybe Ward would lead him to the Batboy. So he bugged Ward's car with a homing device— he'd spent five years in the Army, Royal Engineers, and he knew all about electronic devices. He followed Ward, intended pushing him and the kid over a cliff up near Seahouses. Fortunately, he got interrupted.'

The Chief Constable was silent for a little while. He scratched at his chin, doubtfully.

'You say you'd have got hold of all this, *eventually.* How?'

Charlie Spate hesitated. 'Jack Tenby, sir. He'd got wind of the affair between Carrie Fane and Preece. He made his own enquiries and was going to put his own muscle in once he got his hands on Carrie—she'd done a runner down to London by then. But he was . . . persuaded to let me handle it.'

'By which time,' the Chief Constable suggested sarcastically, 'it was all over anyway.'

Charlie kept his mouth tightly closed.

'And how was it that you . . . *persuaded* Tenby to give you this information?' the Chief Constable asked warily. 'Or shouldn't I ask?'

Charlie thought of Ludmila Paderewski from Russland. He could have nailed Mad Jack Tenby there. But he'd given it away to solve a murder. Which would have been sorted anyway. It annoyed him, but it was too late now. 'Like you keep saying, sir,' he suggested doggedly. 'Mr Tenby is a reformed character. He gave me the information . . . as a public service.'

There was a long silence. The Chief Constable watched him with the stain of suspicion in his eyes. At last, he said, 'I can't say I'm happy, DCI Spate. There's too many loose ends in all this. You'll recall I disciplined DI Connelly for overstepping the mark. Just be careful. I'll be watching you . . .'

Charlie was in a bad temper when he went

back to his office. He banged around his room, kicking the furniture for a while. He felt the Fates had not been kind to him. He wasn't getting the credit he deserved. There was a tap on the door. Elaine Start stood there. She had great legs and a great bosom. And a worried look on her face.

'So?'

She hesitated. 'Terry Bell, guv.'

'What about it?'

'He's done a runner again.'

'*What?*'

Hurriedly, she said, 'They had him in the dock this morning, head bandage and all, at the magistrates court. Mr Ward was there with him: it was a bail application on the outstanding robbery charge. Mr Ward was making the case that in view of the assistance Bell had given in the Preece business, leniency should be shown by the bench. But the magistrates weren't having it—and then the kid suddenly started wriggling through the wood-laminate slats around the dock. You know it's a new, state-of-the-art court they got there now.'

Charlie Spate stared at her, open-mouthed. 'Those slats, they can't be more than seven inches apart.'

'He wriggled through them,' she insisted nervously. 'He got through, went sprawling over the dock and the magistrates bench. He landed up on that speckled green carpet they got there, you know? Just by the press desk. There was no police officer in court—'

'Because the security has been privatised—'

'And the Group 4 guards seemed to have somehow got locked down below in the cell block. Mr Ward, it seems, made a grab at him, got hold of his jumper, but he was out of it like a snake out of its skin.'

Something was bubbling in Charlie Spate's chest.

Lamely, Elaine Start went on, 'He dashed out into the corridor, ducked into the tea room and then went out through the window. Dropped into the road. Everybody went rushing out after him into the street. No sign of him. They think now he probably hid out for a while in that disused church over the road. Behind the pews. Anyway, they scrambled a helicopter—'

'A *helicopter*?' Charlie giggled. He couldn't help himself.

Elaine Start was struggling herself. She managed to keep her face straight, but only just. 'They reckon the manhunt will be over by nightfall. They'll get him again behind bars.'

'*Manhunt*?' Charlie howled. He sat down, laughing. He couldn't help it; in a moment, she had joined him.

Charlie had a vision of the scrawny youngster, emerging from the disused church, showing two fingers to a blind, circling helicopter. 'The little bugger,' Charlie said,

254

wiping his eyes.

When he had calmed down, she was still standing in the doorway, a broad smile on her face. She had great legs. Temptation touched him once more. 'What was that you said to Mad Jack Tenby the other day, about . . . *The Great Gatsby*? Was that another Alan Ladd western?'

She looked at him pityingly. 'It was a love story. Of a doomed kind.' She hesitated, shaking her head. 'You really ought to get out more.'

Charlie smiled. 'Is that an offer?' he asked.